SCRAPE THE GLASS

SCRAPE THE GLASS

MATT RIEDLE

Riverfront Publishing

RPSTL

This book is an original publication of Riverfront Publishing.
Post Office Box 775367, St. Louis, Missouri 63177

Library of Congress Cataloging-in-Publication Data is available upon request.

INTERNATIONAL EDITION ISBN 978-0-9977489-8-7

Printed in the United States of America
10 9 8 7 6 5 4 3 2 1

RPSTL

SCRAPE THE GLASS

One

My Tuesday morning was uneventful, but life has a way of quickly transforming. I could have never imagined what the rest of the day would bring, let alone, the week and the month. As for the month, it was December. December in Denver. I spent my days within the imposing shadows of the snow-covered Front Range. Hidden. Hopefully unseen.

And now, Elsie was unresponsive.

I'd texted her after my second-hour class, but she still hadn't replied. That never happened. She was usually quick to respond. At the latest, she would reply within an hour or two. Or maybe she was simply busy and would get back to me later, but I had an odd feeling that something was wrong.

My fears would soon be confirmed.

I called her phone, mentally preparing to hear it ring, but an automated message replied, "*Ding, ding, ding.* The wireless number you have dialed is no longer in service."

What?

I double-checked to make sure that I'd clicked on the correct contact. *Yup.* There she was: Els. Simple. I'd had her saved as Els since the day we met.

I stared at her name, trying to rationalize why her number was no longer in service. Maybe there had been a glitch.

Students were now filtering into my seventh hour class, raising the volume with each passing second. The sounds were grating. The stench of teen sweat and hormones mixed with cheap fragrances also filled the air.

I tried calling her again, casting glances around my classroom, hoping that I'd get through to Elsie this time.

Nope. Same result.

I was running out of time before my next class began. There wasn't much else I could try to do, anyway. She hadn't returned my text. Her phone had been disconnected.

I thought of another way of reaching her. *Facebook.* I opened the Facebook app on my phone.

At the top of the page, I searched: "Elsie Morton." I was surprised that she didn't immediately pop up as a suggestion. She should have. We had been friends since a few days after we met.

I'd chatted with her much more than anyone else on Messenger. Well, I had, anyway.

Actually, there was another young woman that was at the top of my Messenger list.

After searching, the results populated. My eyes quickly scanned the top results. I didn't see her. I didn't even see anyone with the exact name. The closest matches were a couple of results for "*Elise* Morton."

Had Elsie deleted her Facebook page? Maybe she had grown tired of the constant stream of irrelevance and time-wasting. It was possible, but considering that her phone had also been disconnected … My stomach sank at my next thought.

Did she block me?

But why in the hell would Elsie block me from Facebook? What could I have done to provoke such a drastic response? To actually delete me from social media?

Oh, yeah. That. And the other thing.

But there's no way she could have found out. Well, she could have. But when would she have been able to between this morning and now? How could our relationship have unraveled in the span of a few hours? And then I thought back to another relationship that had unraveled within seconds. There was no coming back from that one.

Never.

For some reason, I looked at Elsie's contact page on my phone. I somehow hadn't noticed it before—probably because I'd been on autopilot, but her contact picture wasn't there.

What the …?

I clicked on the placeholder picture icon, just to be sure.

Nothing. Just a simple "E."

I went to edit her profile so that I could add her picture. Right now, I needed to see her smile. I needed some reassurance that everything was okay between us. Or, more importantly, that *she* was okay.

I went to my images folder to find another picture of her. I scrolled … And scrolled … I'd had dozens, if not hundreds of pictures of Elsie, but suddenly, I couldn't find anything. The last picture I'd taken with her was when we were at dinner the weekend before, but it wasn't there.

I'd also organized some pictures into albums. I looked for the one from our recent weekend in Breckenridge. The album was there, along with pictures of me, but there were absolutely no pictures of Elsie.

What in the …?

While I'd never open the album while in school, I also saw the album cover for the *other* album I had of her. Once again, all I saw was the default placeholder image. Every picture in the album titled "*Bad Els*" had been deleted.

I was now in beyond-panic mode.

"Hey, Mr. Wallace," Michelle Long said. She was a great student, always on top of things.

"Hey," I said, trying to flash a smile.

I looked around the room, finally realizing that all of my students were in my classroom. I also realized that I'd had my head in the phone for the last several minutes, oblivious to the world around me.

Had the bell already rung?

Could I have possibly missed the bell ringing? Possibly, if I had been in such an obstructing daze. It's amazing what people can miss when their focus is captured. Kind of like how we can drive for hours without remembering any details.

"Did the bell ring?" I finally asked, trying to pull myself back into reality, back into my classroom.

Several students laughed.

"Yeah, about three minutes ago," Ally Sedlacek said, grinning. "Didn't you hear it? It's umm, *pretty* loud."

Ally laughed, as did many of the other students.

I quickly regained my bearings and tried my best to laugh along with my students.

"Sorry, boys and girls," I said. "It's been a long day."

I scanned the room. Nobody seemed to care. I was still their teacher, and it's not like it mattered. There might have been a slightly awkward moment, but they probably just figured I was busy. Teachers have had worse lapses …

Did Elsie find out about my lapse? Did she block me?

Where are her pictures?

The thoughts rattled in my head during my last two classes. I'd pulled it together just enough to get through the rest of the day. I'd see Elsie when I got home. That was my solace. After I made it back to our apartment, everything would be back to normal. There was surely a logical explanation for all of this.

Maybe there had been some crazy glitch with my phone. That would explain everything. Maybe I'd stop by AT&T after talking to Elsie. She was probably just as worried about me.

That's what I tried to consciously tell myself, but underneath everything, I was a wreck. It was one thing if she simply hadn't texted me back. I'm not insecure enough for that to make me sweat. But her phone was not in service? *And* her Facebook profile was gone? *AND* all of her pictures had been deleted from my phone? It made zero sense.

During the drive home, despite trying to reassure myself that everything was okay, I mentally braced myself for what I would find. I almost knew that Elsie wouldn't be there. If by chance she was, then I had a feeling that it wouldn't go well.

I was really holding out hope for a phone malfunction.

And then the thought reentered my mind, one that made me almost vomit: What if something had happened to her? What if someone had kidnapped her and deleted every trace of her? I still didn't understand how all of her pictures could be deleted from my phone. That was the most troubling aspect.

Could I have been hacked?

Without realizing it, I was already on my street: *Walker Lane.* It was contained within a cozy neighborhood on Denver's south side. I shared an apartment with Elsie, or maybe you could call it a condo. I didn't see any difference.

I also didn't see Elsie's car.

Two

Elsie wasn't home yet, but that wasn't a huge deal. Sure, she usually made it home well before me but not always. Sometimes, she'd sit at Starbucks for a few hours in the evening, taking in the sights and sounds, the intoxicating aroma of roasted coffee beans. At least that's what she'd always told me.

I took a deep breath, trying to compose myself before opening the door and taking the stairs to our second-story unit. This was all usually done without any preparation or second thought, but this afternoon, everything was taking more effort. My stomach was in knots, and I felt a little nauseated.

I needed to get moving. Maybe there would be answers upstairs. I was able to open the common landing door with my key.

Sometimes, after opening the door, I'd hear Elsie moving around upstairs. Not today.

I climbed the carpeted stairs, already sliding into nostalgia mode—thinking back through our memories together. How we'd met shortly after I'd moved to Colorado, after I had sought my much-needed fresh start. After I'd left my regrettable memories back in Missouri.

And there she had been, like she was out there waiting for me the entire time. *Elsie Morton.* A woman who shared so many of my interests. She had skied from a young age, and I'd started snowboarding as soon as I'd arrived in Colorado. We also both loved to camp, hike, and watch Broncos games.

But what really got me about Elsie was her mind. There were parts that she never took me to, but that's what made her all the more intriguing. I knew she was damaged to some degree. Something had happened to her. Something long ago. I know this because she dreamed about it.

Violent dreams.

Maybe her dreams had somehow surfaced. Or maybe they'd grown too much for her to bear.

Before I knew it, I'd opened the door to our condo. My steps were slow and beleaguered. If Elsie were there, I surely would have already heard her. I was delaying the inevitable.

But maybe she was sleeping. *And had somehow made it home without her car.* Maybe she'd had a wreck and had to be dropped off. And maybe, just maybe, the wreck had caused her Facebook page to be deleted and her phone to be disconnected.

I shuffled through our living area, past the kitchen to the left, down the hall, and into the bedroom. It was the room with the strongest energy of our time together.

My eyes scanned the room first. Nothing. There was almost nothing at all. Yeah, there was a bed, dresser, and nightstands, but it seemed unusually bare. I felt like I might pass out; I needed support. I sank into the bed, pushing my hands into the red and black comforter.

I continued to look around the room. *No Elsie.* It also seemed emptier, but I wasn't sure how. Isn't it crazy how a cursory review can leave so much hidden?

"Elsie?" I asked aloud, not a whisper, not a yell. I used the same volume as if someone had been sitting next to me. I didn't know what effect this would have. It wasn't like I was trying to keep this plea hidden from someone. Maybe I just wanted to hear her name.

No response, but I didn't expect there to be. Maybe if I took a nap, maybe this would all disappear. Was it possible that this was all a crazy dream? Had I somehow shifted to a parallel reality? Would there be any way of shifting back?

No, it's just a dream. Yet it all felt so real ... Then again, people have had far more vivid dreams.

Oh, Elsie, where have you gone?

My cursory glance was about to turn into a deeper search. I think I'd put it off because I already knew what I would find.

Up until then, I was holding out hope that she was late getting home and that my phone had malfunctioned. Or maybe she had simply left me, blocked my number and blocked me from Facebook. But that still didn't explain the deleted pictures.

It took a concerted effort, but I climbed to my feet. I walked over to her dresser and pulled open the top drawer.

I frowned. Yeah, I had to be dreaming.

It was empty. The chocolate-walnut bottom stared back at me, taunting me. I scoffed and shook my head. Bewildered. I opened the second drawer, same thing. The third, same. The fourth, nothing. She had emptied everything.

What in the …?

I stumbled backward, reaching for the bed, my eyes glued to the dresser. It was all gone. When I stumbled into the bed, I sat down. Everything else in the room looked like it was in order. The TV, end tables, and dressers. The curtains were pulled tightly closed in front of the windows.

The heater kicked on.

My ears and eyes followed the hum to the heating ducts by our walk-in closet. Curiously, I walked over to the closet, stepping over my pants and shirt from the day before. Only my clothes. I didn't see anything of Elsie's. No scrubs. No bras. Now I realized exactly why the room had seemed so empty.

Fatigue and confusion intermingled. A sense of disbelief. Almost apathy. I simply didn't believe that this was happening.

Yes, I had to be dreaming.

The closet door was propped open slightly. I didn't even want to look. Without looking, I knew her side was empty, but I needed to be sure. I needed to torture myself more.

I took a deep breath and pushed the door open.

One side was full of clothes, primarily slacks, shirts, and ties. The other side … a few hangers. Nothing else. Not even a left-over shirt that she never wore.

She took it all.

I stared at the bare white wall, which should have been blocked by her clothes. I'd initially been too dazed to respond in any meaningful way, but I was beginning to wake up to reality. The truth was sinking in … Elsie had left me. But I still didn't know what to think or what to do next.

I might have always seen it coming, but not like this. Without any kind of warning? Without saying anything? Deleting me and blocking me from everything? Also, it would have taken hours to take everything out of here. When had she done it? She must have circled back to our place after I'd left in the morning.

I thought back to what Elsie had said the night before at dinner, about how much she loved me. I remembered how she had looked at me, with such determination.

Or was it loathing?

Her looks were loathing. She took her clothing.

I actually laughed, and it took me a minute to stop.

It couldn't have been loathing. She had been playful before bed. I'd go back to that night many times, searching for clues. The night before I lost her. I'd wonder if I could have changed what happened. Maybe if I'd said something different or hugged her a little tighter. Or should I have given her space? Would any of that have made a difference? Probably not, but maybe.

There's no use thinking about it because I'll never know.

Thinking back to last night, we had settled down for bed a little after eleven. She had a twelve-hour shift beginning at six. I had another week of school beginning at Washington High. I'd considered staying up to finish my lesson plan, but I figured I'd have time after Elsie left.

I already knew that I wouldn't be able to get back to sleep after she left since I never could.

She snuggled into my arms, throwing her behind into my manhood. Grinding a little. We actually both had pajamas on, but it didn't completely dull the sensation.

"Baby," I mumbled, feeling super drowsy.

"Yeah?" she asked mischievously.

"You have to wake up in a few hours, you know?"

"Yeah?" she said. "I know." She hadn't stopped grinding.

"Then maybe you should stop teasing both of us. You're just going to get yourself worked up and you know how that goes … I'm beat. I could fall asleep any second."

She stopped grinding and didn't say anything. That's not always the best response from a woman.

Shit … Silence prevailed, with our breathing occasionally filling the gaps. The glow from our alarm clock was the only light in the room. I could see the time over Elsie's head: 11:28.

"Els? You asleep?"

"Yup," she said, scooting a few inches away.

I leaned over and kissed the side of her neck, whispering "Goodnight" into her ear.

"Night," she said. "I love you, Mark. Always."

I thought of the last few weeks before responding. I thought of what I'd been doing. I thought of *her*. It really didn't take more than a split-second to consider, not long enough to make Elsie wonder or doubt my feelings.

"Love you, too."

What seemed like seconds later, our bedside alarm clock went off. I swore that I had just fallen asleep. They say that time always flies when you're moving toward an undesirable event.

That couldn't have been more accurate.

That next morning, I'd been primed and ready to go. I may have been too tired the night before, but in the morning, yeah, that was another story. But Elsie had already been up for a while. She was in the bathroom getting ready for work. I'd watched her from the bed, not knowing that it might be the last time.

Back in the present, I pushed the vision of Elsie getting ready from my mind. This time, when I looked toward the bathroom, nobody was there.

I sighed and walked over to the window, pushing the velvety, crimson curtains aside.

If it were a typical evening, her Infiniti SUV would already be parked between my Chevy Cruze and the sign that said "No Parking to Corner." She was always in the front-of-the-line, well-situated to easily blast off. In the middle of the night—without anyone knowing. Except this time, she must have pulled the same trick in the middle of the day. I tried to picture her lugging all of her clothes down the steps.

I couldn't do it. It didn't make sense.

I continued to stare out the window. From my perch, I had a commanding view of Walker Street. A line of barren trees stood just below the window, between our apartment building and the road.

An unbroken line of two-story homes stood across the street. The homes probably cost three times more than our units. They were all gated with small front yards.

Instinctively, my eyes flicked to the home directly across the street. No movement. I must admit that this was also my morning routine, after Elsie left. I'd watch for movement at one particular building.

Nothing.

I shifted my focus to our side of the street. My car was right where it should be, probably parked too far from the curb. I'd had other things on my mind when I'd come home today.

There was nothing in front of my Chevy … No car, no truck, no Infiniti SUV. No Elsie.

I pressed my forehead against the window and gave myself a hug. I wouldn't cry. I couldn't do it, and I didn't deserve to.

Elsie was gone, and despite trying to blame her or someone else, I knew that it was my fault.

I shouldn't have lied to her.

Three

I turned away from the window, walking back through the bedroom. I remembered the night I had met Elsie. It was the middle of summer, but in the middle of the mountains at ten thousand feet of elevation, it never gets too hot. We had run into each other at a dive bar in Leadville. She had sparkled like the sun radiating off of a glacial lake. She had the same eyes as those lakes—that greenish-blue. Her eyes glistened and her blonde hair bounced around her face as she laughed.

She had caught my gaze, held it for a second, then quickly turned away. It almost looked like she had wanted to run. I was sure she had been receptive, though. I wanted to approach her, but not if she was going to take off running and screaming into the cool Colorado night. Then again, if I hung back, I probably wouldn't ever muster the courage to approach her.

As they say, he who hesitates, masturbates.

I hadn't turned away yet, and before I could, she slowly turned back toward me, a weak smile overtaking her face. I grinned slightly, barely perceptible, and made my approach.

While I walked toward her, she ran her fingers through her hair. As I came closer, I realized her eyes were green, maybe hazel. Sometimes it's hard to tell. Sometimes eyes change color. It doesn't matter anyway. All I knew was that they continued to dazzle. That's what mattered most. She was only a few inches shorter than me, but the top of her voluminous hair was nearly even with the top of my head.

The band was just getting into their rendition of "Wagon Wheel" by the Old Crow Medicine Show.

"Hey," I said, finally getting close enough to talk to her. The walk over to this woman seemed like it had taken hours, leaving my legs a little rubbery. "What's your name?"

"Elsie," she said, her smile widening. I imagined her saying her name with such pride as a young girl. When we don't have anything else in life, we always have our name. It's the first thing that's given to us, and it can live on forever.

"What's yours?" she asked.

"Mark," I said, holding out my hand.

She initially made no movement to shake my hand. Instead, she bit her lip and looked down at my right hand, hesitating.

"Nice to meet you, Mark," she said, finally reaching for my

outstretched hand. I'd nearly given up and pulled it back due to the awkwardness. And then, I lost her for several seconds. She continued to look at me, but her eyes were distant, covered with a glaze of longing.

Maybe. I had no idea what she was thinking.

"Nice to meet you, too," I said, hoping it would bring her back to me. She shook her head and regained her smile, as if her lapse hadn't happened.

Back in the present, I tried to smile at the memory of meeting her, but instead, it made me feel worse. I was near tears. Remembering how it once was, how it might never be again. *If she had truly left me.* Or were my building tears actually from shame or regret?

I quickly thought back to that initial giddiness between us— that instant spark. How we made out in the dive bar's grimy bathroom later that night ...

The bathroom.

Had she taken all of her bathroom things? All of her makeup, shampoo, conditioner, body soap, feminine products, straightener, curler, and whatever else she had in there ... her freaking toothbrush.

Did she take her toothbrush?

I did an about-face near the bedroom door, turning back to the master bathroom. The door was wide-open. From my angle, I could see a solitary blue towel hanging on the rack.

My towel. And absolutely nothing else.

I wasn't sure it even mattered at this point. What if her

toothbrush were there? Her clothes were all gone, her car was gone, her pictures were gone, and she was gone.

What would I do with a freaking toothbrush?

I'd have hope.

Just as I'd expected, the bathroom had been cleaned out. Electronic toothbrush and all. It was eye-opening to remember just how bare a bathroom could look. It was a flashback to my bachelor days, back in Soulard.

Back before I had to leave St. Louis.

I grabbed my toothbrush from its holder, knocking it over in the process. It fell into the sink, clanking loudly as it tumbled. I picked it up and ran the brush under the water, leaving the water running. Elsie had convinced me to turn the water off while I brushed.

But she wasn't here now.

For the next several minutes, I brushed my teeth. I didn't know what else to do. It didn't make sense. Elsie had disappeared, with everything. Her clothes, her bags, her shoes, all of her bathroom things. Everything.

Except for me. She had left me.

I wanted to call the hospital to see if she had made it to work this morning, but it was still so soon—they might think I'm a crazy, creepy stalker. Maybe I would call in the morning.

I thought back to her taste in clothing and accessories, the six-dollar Starbucks drinks that she purchased twice daily. Her money went out as quickly as it came in.

When we met, I couldn't believe the money that she casually

spent during the course of a day, in a week. If I wanted coffee, I drove through McDonald's. A large for a dollar? You can't beat that. Hell, it's arguably cheaper than the time spent making it yourself. And most days, I took my lunch to work. Saving twenty-to-thirty dollars per day adds up fast.

Maybe she could sell a couple of her handbags to make a buck or two. Or she could sell her Infiniti. She claimed that it was paid off. I wasn't sure how. She made decent money, but a new Infiniti SUV is a seventy-thousand-dollar vehicle. I thought she had bought it brand new, but maybe it had been used. I couldn't remember. It still would have been at least thirty or forty thousand dollars.

I turned the bathroom light off. Once again, the only glow came from the alarm clock: *7:33*.

There was no way so much time had passed. I'd already been home for two hours? *Impossible.*

I really didn't want to start over again … It's tiring to put yourself out there, meet women you actually give a damn about, whittle away their defenses (let down yours), and learn who they really are.

You might think you know a person, but then they leave you in the middle of the day. People will lie, and not always to hurt you, but to protect you. Maybe she just wanted to avoid a fight. Maybe she thought this was the easiest way to let me go.

Was it a cowardly solution? Yes. But if that were the case, at least it had a basis in compassion, however flawed. Or maybe I was being selfish? There was no way of knowing.

Not yet.

A quick pass through the rest of the house didn't uncover anything of significance. It was now dark, though, so I didn't notice much as I walked down the hallway. I stepped past the spare bedroom which we had turned into an office, past the other bathroom.

Our kitchen and dining area opened up into the living room. Two square columns stood between the two areas, with the kitchen standing to my right. We generally ate at the bar or lounging on the couch. We didn't have a table.

That's a lie. We had a (nice) card table that we brought out in the rare event that someone else came over. Otherwise, she had concluded that the space was too small. And she had convinced me that we should fill the limited space we had with the living room furniture.

It all looked so empty today. Yet, at the same time, I had plenty of room to breathe.

Four

Elsie returned at some point during that Colorado night.

I was surprised that I was able to rest so comfortably. I'd feared that the guilt would consume me. Not only the guilt, but the regret. My sheets enveloped me, and I was out within minutes. Maybe seconds. It had been such an exhausting day; it was easy to allow my biological need for sleep to overcome my stress.

Elsie was in every dream.

Most of the dreams were innocent and actually refreshing. In one, she was getting ready for work. I lay in bed watching her in front of the mirror. She must have thought I was sleeping because she tiptoed around the room, careful not to make a noise. But I watched her. I was entranced. I couldn't look away. This might have been more of a memory than a dream. It was one of my favorite memories of Els—watching her when she didn't know it. She would let her guard down and allow her true self to shine through.

She was lightly humming an old Bruno Mars song, twisting her hips. She'd also dance when I was watching, but she was never quite as loose, always with a hint of reservation. She wasn't making much noise, just enough.

In another dream, we were at a Broncos football game. We were the only people in attendance. We sat at the fifty-yard line, twelve yards up. *I'd kill for those tickets.* Snow swirled around us, but it had to be eighty degrees. Sweat rolled down my face, down my back. I'd try to take off layers of clothing, but it didn't help. Elsie just sat there looking at me, a curious grin on her face, like she was dying to tell me the funniest joke of all time.

Those two dreams were innocent enough unless I was missing some deeper message. They say that all of our dreams are projections of our subconscious mind. *They* say a lot of things though. I've had dreams that mean absolutely nothing.

But I knew exactly what the third dream had meant . . . It was a memory from all of those years ago back in St. Louis. The night that *she* had died.

Before I could slip too deeply into it, my alarm went off.

Admitting the disappearance of a loved one is difficult. Despite the absence of all of Elsie's belongings, I wanted to believe that she would come back to me—or be returned. Whatever.

It was definitely a blow.

Had she simply not come home, then it might have been easier. Maybe. But considering everything was gone? All of her pictures deleted from my phone? I couldn't deal with it. It was all so unprecedented. Unexplainable. They don't put out manuals or YouTube videos for this scenario.

Before anyone could help me, I would have to admit that she was gone. Missing. No, *misplaced*. She was simply misplaced. She would return. She just needed to be found. I could accept that. I needed help finding my misplaced girlfriend.

I sighed and pulled on a pair of basketball shorts. They might have been dirty, but it didn't matter.

I walked into the kitchen. The digital clock on the stove showed that it was already past six. Ordinarily, it would be time for Elsie to be at work. I wanted to call Arapahoe Memorial, but I stalled. I wouldn't call. Not yet. I didn't want to hear that she wasn't there. I didn't want further confirmation that she wasn't with me anymore.

Instead, I walked over to the couch and collapsed. If I'd become dead to her, then I might as well be dead to the world. Maybe with a little more sleep, I'd be better equipped to handle her disappearance and whatever would follow.

People would ask questions. My heartbeat quickened at the thought. My stomach clenched.

The hospital, her family, her friends …

The police.

I'd have to report her missing at some point. I'd have to

speak with uniformed officers, detectives, and the entire crew. I wasn't sure if I could handle that. I would need to ensure that I had all of my stories straight.

Plus, I didn't want to file the report right away. That might look bad. They might wonder why I was so sure that she was missing. After less than a day.

Does he know something? Did he do it? Did he murder her and bury her in a landfill? An old quarry?

Maybe that was an illogical train of thought, but I wanted to ensure that I didn't slip up at any turn. I'd successfully avoided criminal charges sticking the last time I was in a similar situation.

Then again, if I waited too long, that would probably look worse. I'd give myself until evening—give Elsie until evening. That would be twenty-four hours since I discovered her missing (*misplaced*), and it would give me enough time to perform some due diligence, though I didn't have any concrete idea.

I couldn't help but wonder if this was all some kind of cosmic karma. Maybe one unforgivable act had finally caught up with me. It had been years, but I didn't know how long the karmic statute of limitations extended.

Just go back to sleep.

But I couldn't. I needed to call the hospital. I couldn't put this off any longer. If I knew that Elsie was okay, that would at least give me some comfort. It would hurt like hell, but at least she'd be okay. I didn't want to even consider other possibilities of where she might be.

I finally bit the bullet and called the hospital.

A man answered.

"Good morning, Arapahoe Memorial. How may I direct your call?"

"I'm not sure," I said, already threatening to stumble over my words. "I wanted to make sure that someone made it there this morning."

"Alrighty. I might be able to help you with that. What is the patient's name?"

"Sorry, she's not a patient. She works there."

He briefly hesitated, probably wondering if he would blow someone's cover, but he continued. "Which department does she work in? I could connect you."

I had to think for a minute. We didn't talk much about the hospital. I'd dated other nurses who wanted to discuss every-thing—all of the tragic stories about the steady stream of death. But not Elsie. She would generally come home and turn that part of her life off. Like a switch.

But then I remembered. "Radiology," I said. "Sorry, it slipped my mind for a second."

He transferred me. As I waited for radiology to answer, I wondered if Elsie had experienced something awful at the hospital. Maybe she could no longer cope with the stress. Had I not been there for her? Maybe I should have asked more questions about her job. I should have let her unload everything. Hell, I probably should have also had sex with her the other night.

My thoughts were interrupted.

"Radiology. This is Trisha."

"Yes, hello," I said.

"Hello? How may I help you, sir?"

I had to risk sounding like the possessive, scorned boyfriend. "I was just wondering if Elsie Morton made it to work yesterday or today." *Silence.* I continued. "I'm her boyfriend, and, um, she didn't make it home after work yesterday. I've waited for her to show up, but she's still missing. I think. I'm honestly not sure what happened, but I just wanted to see if she's been at work."

"Elsie Morton?" she asked.

"Yeah, Elsie Morton."

"Hmmm. That name doesn't sound familiar. Do you have the right department?" She became *more* critical. "You said you are her boyfriend?"

"Yeah," I said. "She doesn't like to talk about work. She likes to leave it at the door."

"Man, I understand that," Trisha said. "Tell you what: I'll look her up on the hospital roster and get back to you. What's your phone number?"

I gave her my number and hung up. My heartbeat had increased. I hoped I'd been mistaken about her department. She might have said radiology, but she might have said pediatrics. *Maybe her friend worked in radiology.* That was possible. The only trouble was, she never discussed any friends at the hospital.

Not that I remembered, anyway.

Maybe I should have paid more attention during dinner the night before. I knew something had been off. I thought back to the way that Elsie's eyes pierced through me, yet she was so distant. Then again, she had been flirty later that night.

There was something she said though, something that finally came bubbling back up. I wasn't sure why I hadn't considered it earlier. Maybe it was a combination of the shock and fatigue.

"I've been happy here," she had said, after pushing away her barely-touched plate of shrimp scampi.

"Same," I said, devouring my last bite of filet.

And then Elsie had smiled. A sad smile.

"I wish everything could last, but it's all so fleeting."

I'd swallowed hard, not sure where she was going with that thought, but maybe I should have been more reassuring.

"The best things last," I'd said. "Right?"

"I guess," she'd said, and that was about the end of that.

We had changed the topic to sharing a dessert, and the tone of the evening became more positive. Maybe that's why I hadn't given it much further thought yet. The comment was a little out there, but it wasn't anything seriously alarming.

Now, I wondered if I had missed something. Should I have pulled more information out of her? She had been so cryptic, but again, it had quickly passed.

Suddenly, my phone rang, interrupting my thoughts.

"Mark Wallace," I said, lying back on the bed.

"Mark, this is Trisha with radiology at Arapahoe Memorial."

"Yes?"

"Okay, sir. I checked with the other departments, and I'm not sure how to put this, but…"

The silence was brief, but it almost drove me insane.

"Tell me," I quickly demanded.

"We have no record of a woman named 'Elsie Morton' ever working at Arapahoe Memorial."

Five

My jaw went slack. I closed my eyes. *Too surreal.* I must have misheard the receptionist. Ordinarily, this would have been beyond comprehension, but after the events of the last day or two, I honestly wasn't too surprised. Then again, there was no way Elsie didn't work there.

"Sir? Did you hear what I said? We have no record of Elsie Morton ever working here."

"Excuse me?" I said, finally snapping back to *reality.*

"I'm sorry, but your *girlfriend* doesn't work here," she said, not hiding her cynicism. "We don't even have an 'Elsie' working here. There is a man named Jerry Morton in janitorial services, but I doubt that helps you."

After a brief pause, she continued. "Is there anything else I can help you with, sir?"

I couldn't help but notice a hint of humor in her voice. If I was on the other end of the line, I might have also thought it was pretty damn funny—some guy who was probably given fake information from a girl who didn't want to see him. Or that I probably wasn't anywhere close to her boyfriend. Maybe a guy that she had met at the bar and talked to for a week.

But here I was, on *my* end, and I was experiencing a polar opposite emotion. I was almost tempted to lay into her, but I relented. Maybe she was an incompetent receptionist. Maybe she hadn't searched the entire directory. It had to somehow be her fault. She couldn't have been telling me the truth.

But instead, I relented. I trusted her. Right now, I trusted her more than I trusted Elsie.

"No, that's all. Thanks," I finally muttered, immediately ending the call. I didn't want to hear another word. The shame and embarrassment were too much. But I also felt an insane level of hurt and confusion. All negative emotions. And negative emotions never get a person anywhere positive.

Elsie did not work at Arapahoe. Had she lied to me or had I confused the hospitals? I was sure she had said Arapahoe, that she had always said Arapahoe, even when most people would simply say "work." *Mark, I'm still at Arapahoe, can you pick up pizza? Arapahoe called me in on Sunday. Fuck Arapahoe!*

It was such a unique name, not so much in the Denver area, but it was still something that I knew I'd remember correctly. Or maybe she was on staff somewhere else but also worked at Arapahoe. Maybe some kind of contract work? I wasn't sure if nurses did that. I thought they did. Maybe something like the traveling nurses or nurses on some kind of rotation.

Or hell, maybe she worked at Arapahoe Basin, the ski resort out in Summit County.

My phone was still pressed to my cheek. I let it slide down my chest. It tumbled onto the bed next to me. I'd considered throwing it against the wall, shattering it into hundreds of pieces, but it wasn't the phone's fault. I knew it would make me feel better, but only temporarily and at what cost?

Had Elsie seriously lied to me about where she worked? That wouldn't make any sense. People only lie about where they work if they are unemployed, underemployed, or to impress someone. Could she have been some gas station attendant who wanted to woo me by saying she was a nurse?

That didn't explain her new Infiniti. It didn't explain the thousands of dollars that she tore through every month.

Actually, nothing explained that. It was something that I'd always wondered. Over time, I gradually accepted that she had money that she never discussed. Maybe a large inheritance that she didn't want to share with me. Or maybe it simply wasn't a lot of money to her ...

Who are you, Elsie?

I was holding out hope that she worked at another hospital, but something already told me that she didn't. Nonetheless, I cranked up Google, and I found phone numbers for all the hospitals within the Denver metro. I wasn't taking any chances.

Elsie Morton? Let me check ... Sorry, sir.

We have no record of an Elsie Morton ever working here.

And so it went. Elsie Morton had never worked at any of the hospitals in Denver. I paced the bedroom calling them all: Denver Health, Porter Adventist, Rose Medical, National Jewish Health, University of Colorado Anschutz, among others. Nothing. I even checked the hospitals in Boulder and several other cities within an hour or two.

It was getting to the point where I was embarrassed to call. I'd spent at least an hour looking up the numbers and calling the hospitals. I'd usually be placed on hold, sometimes they would be critical, wondering if I was a stalker, perhaps a former patient who fell hard for a nurse and couldn't get her to return his calls or raise the puppy he had sent her. I wouldn't be able to blame them if they didn't want to give out her information, even if she legitimately worked there.

There *is* malevolence in this world. There *are* men out there who will hurt women.

With that thought, finally, I sighed and gave up and plugged my phone into my charger. I placed it on the nightstand, next to Elsie's alarm clock. The alarm was still set for four, when she always wakes up. Seeing her alarm clock set to four helped ground my perception of reality. After all, she *was* here. Right? Yes, I knew she had been living with me.

At least she had left the alarm clock.

Then again, that alarm clock could have been anyone's. There weren't any distinguishing features, yet I knew that it had been hers.

But how?

Fingerprints? Yes, she had surely left her fingerprints on the alarm clock. How would I be able to verify that? I'd almost have to call the cops. I had a sinking feeling, what would the cops find out about her? What would they try to pin on me? And what would happen when they dug into my history?

I couldn't deal with those thoughts now.

I tumbled back onto the bed, looking up at the stationary fan. It was a nice fixture—I thought so, anyway, but Elsie had always complained about it. She had wanted me to spruce it up.

Elsie had always wanted the finest in life. It was a wonder that she stuck around with a high school teacher.

Well ... At least she'd stuck around for a little while.

I closed my eyes. Surely, I needed to report her disappearance. But if she wasn't working at Arapahoe, I couldn't say that she didn't make it to work. They'd immediately ask me where she worked. I'd tell them. They'd call Arapahoe. The cops would think that I was insane, or that I was hiding something.

They would also comb the apartment for clues. There was absolutely nothing of Elsie's at my place—*our* place. They would want a picture. All of her pictures had been removed from the apartment or deleted from my phone. They would have had absolutely nothing to go on. I would probably also be committed to the nut house for having an imaginary girlfriend, and then I'd be arrested for making a false report. Hell, at least I'd be able to use an insanity plea.

Unbelievable.

My stomach was churning. It was too much.

I stumbled to the bathroom and vomited into the toilet. While kneeling on the tiled floor, I looked at the shower, at the empty space where her things used to be. I'm not sure how they could have all disappeared so quickly. They were all just *there*. Right *there*. Two days ago, I could have picked up a bottle of her shampoo, made some wisecrack about how she needed four different varieties. In fact, I think that's exactly what I'd done a few days before.

She'd laughed, telling me that I didn't understand women. Well, apparently not. Apparently, there was much more that I needed to learn. For starters, I needed to learn how they could mysteriously vanish into the night—or afternoon, whatever.

I heaved once or twice more. Nothing came out. That wasn't a surprise. I'd barely eaten anything since she left.

I pulled myself back to my feet, weakened by the vomiting. I decided to check the websites of every local news station. Maybe she had died. Or maybe they had uncovered this huge conspiracy where women were infiltrating men's homes, lying about where they worked, siphoning all of the man's savings, hacking and deleting any pictures from the man's phone, and then taking off in the night. Robbing me wouldn't have made any sense though. Elsie had plenty of money, and my savings account was still intact.

Actually, I hadn't checked that yet. Maybe she had robbed me before leaving. *Insane thoughts.*

Nonetheless, before checking the news websites, I logged into my First Bank account, bracing for another shock.

Whew. It was all still there. I checked my TD Ameritrade investing account, same result. Untouched. I had to stop and smile at what I had accumulated.

I had saved $5,000 per year for the last eleven years. I'd done my own investing, making an annualized return of 11.3%. Do the math if you want, but my $55,000 investment had already doubled to roughly $110,000. That's not too shabby on a high school teacher's salary. It helps that I know a little bit about investing, but compound interest is the eighth wonder of the world. It's another one of those quotes that's attributed to Einstein, but I'm not sure whether he said it or not. But yeah, if I stayed on course, I would have a million dollars in eighteen more years. Not a bad retirement. I'd never even missed the money.

Then again, I wasn't sure it would mean anything after all of this. I knew I could find another woman, but this wasn't like Elsie had just left me. I didn't think so, anyway. I really didn't know. It hurt my head to think about.

I closed out of my account and switched gears. The news. I still needed to check the news. I kept getting so distracted, my brain bouncing around with no direction or guidance. Possibly delaying something that would hurt. A self-preservation tactic.

The news.

Maybe I would be able to find answers. Maybe there had

been an accident. I checked all of the affiliates, but I didn't find anything substantial. The Broncos were playing a big game this weekend so that dominated most of the headlines. They were fighting valiantly for a playoff spot, but it looked like the Miami Dolphins might sneak in ahead of them. Not that I really cared at the moment. But it's kind of crazy, even when you're insanely stressed out about something—even something of this magnitude, your focus can be shifted. You can be transported to a completely different frame of mind. All it takes is a distraction or the conscious awareness to shift the focus.

For a split-second, the Broncos news had made me feel like a normal guy. But I kept searching the other news stories… There were some isolated homicides. Thankfully, Denver isn't the south side of Chicago. It has its share of crime, but it's not bad. None of the victims matched Elsie's description, not even close. Not too many 5'7" blonde, white women are victims of random urban homicides. Sure, it happens, but not as often as some of the others.

There was a white man in his teens, a couple of black men in their twenties. Mostly male victims, as usual. Very few white women are actually murdered, even though they steal the headlines when it happens.

All of the stories started to blur together. If I didn't see the buzzwords (blonde, woman, white), I quickly moved on.

I gave up. It wasn't going to help me, anyway.

I needed to call the cops and report Elsie missing, regardless of what the fallout might be. I would be honest and tell them about calling Arapahoe—about what they had told me. That they had no record of an Elsie Morton working there.

I'm sure the cops often dealt with misinformation. The problem would arise if *I* lied to them, or if I didn't call them at all. I knew that if I made any false move—regardless of my intentions, they would pin me as a suspect.

Hell, they probably would regardless.

I thought back to what had happened in St. Louis. I remembered the jail cell. I'd had to stay there for three days before I was finally bonded out.

I hadn't told Elsie about that. It was my past, and I hadn't wanted to alarm her. She didn't need to know about the woman before and what had happened to her. Some secrets are better left unsaid. Truly, it was better for everyone.

That was about all I recounted before falling asleep. That was probably a good thing.

Six

As much as I hated to do it, under the circumstances, I really needed to get back to work. Back to Washington High School. Even calling off one day was rare for me, unless I was taking a vacation or taking the day to go snowboarding.

I woke up to an empty bed for the second straight morning. I'd been hopeful that the previous day had been a dream, but I had no such luck. Elsie wasn't in bed. Her clothes weren't in the closet. There was still absolutely no trace of her. I didn't think her clothes would magically reappear, but I was holding out hope that I'd find something that she left behind. It didn't need to be much, either. Maybe a stray sock or a bobby pin. Anything that confirmed that she had been here.

But I found nothing.

I got up and went through the motions, like it was any other day. I'd somehow need to feign normalcy and resume my role as a high school history teacher, with or without Elsie.

Usually, I arrived at the school at least thirty minutes before the start of my first class. Not today. I made it inside as the warning bell was ringing. This signaled to the students that they had two minutes to make it to class. It had always seemed unnecessary and coddling, but now I was the one who needed the added reminder to be on time.

I picked up my step and turned down the hall toward my classroom. Most of the students had shuffled into their classes by now, but a few stragglers were still roaming the halls. And I noticed another teacher was among them.

Kyle Bellamy, the music teacher, gave me an awkward look. He was young, mid-twenties young. He had a strong presence on TikTok, and all of the girls loved him. He was wearing a bright red Burton snowboarding coat. It looked like he had just come back from Breckenridge.

"Running late, Marky Mark?" he asked.

I loved Mark Wahlberg, but I hated that nickname.

"How did you guess?" I said.

"I'm just a young sleuth like that." Kyle grinned. "Hey, are we still on for poker this week? Your place, right?"

I'd forgotten all about our weekly poker game. All of the guys rotated host duties. I didn't always make it, but I hosted once every two months. That's usually how it went with the other guys … They might not make it every week, but they'd always take hosting seriously. They wouldn't want to let down everyone else.

"Of course," I said, but then I decided to give myself a possible out. "If anything changes, I'll let you guys know."

Kyle leaned in so that nobody else could hear. "Hey, Marky Mark, given the circumstances, it would be understandable if you had to cancel. We wouldn't judge you."

I turned my head to the side, taking in what Kyle had just said. *What in the hell did he mean by that?*

I took a step back, by that time Kyle had also leaned away. We looked at each other. It looked like Kyle was fighting back a smirk, but maybe it was my imagination.

"What do you—"

The second bell rang.

"Shit!" Kyle said. "I better get to class. I wouldn't want to ruin my *stellar reputation* as the exemplary music teacher."

Before I could respond, Kyle had high-stepped it down the hallway and began his march up the stairs.

I was left scratching my head, wondering what Kyle meant, or how he knew anything was amiss. Maybe he had said that simply because I was later than usual. No, that really wouldn't make any sense.

I thought about Elsie during most of the day, where she might be, what might have happened to her. And then I also thought of what Kyle Bellamy had said:

Hey, Marky Mark, given the circumstances, it would be understandable if you had to cancel.

Kyle knew something. How? I had no idea, because I barely even knew anything ...

Oh, well.

I was almost through the day. I'd checked my phone religiously, desperately willing Elsie to call or message me. Nothing. I couldn't focus on anything else.

At the end of my seventh hour class, Ally hung back, eying me curiously. She hesitated a moment before finally approaching my desk with a smile.

All of the other students had left. It was only me and her.

I'd played out this scenario many times before ...

She pushed her jet-black hair behind her ear and smiled, picking up a picture from my desk. "This one is so cute. I love looking at the pictures of your niece and nephew," she said. "What are their names?"

"Ethan and Ella," I said flatly, eying her, then flicking my eyes toward the door, wondering if anyone would come inside.

"Aww, that's adorable," she said, returning the picture to the desk. Her eyes fluttered up to mine. "Why don't you have your own kids?"

I looked back at her and blinked. She had hit me where it hurt. "Just not the right time." I tried to smile, but I couldn't.

"Is your girlfriend too old?"

"What?" I said, sharply. "Ally, that's inappropriate."

She looked shocked and hurt. "I'm sorry, I didn't mean it

like that. I just know that she's a little older and it gets harder after a certain point. Please don't be mad at me."

I felt bad. Maybe I'd overreacted.

"No, no," I said. "Don't worry about it."

Her smile returned.

I continued, but I needed to end the interaction. I couldn't deal with her right now. Not with Elsie missing.

"Ally, did you have a question about the quiz, or...?"

"Oh, yeah," she said, pulling out her quiz.

From my desk, I watched the Vice Principal, Tim Nolan, suddenly appear in the doorway. He leaned against the doorway, watching (judging) me.

Ally flipped her hair and leaned over my desk, pointing to an answer I'd marked wrong.

"All right, let's take a look," I said.

"I'm sorry, I'm kind of dumb, but can you explain this? I don't understand why this answer isn't right."

I glanced from Nolan to Ally—trying not to look down Ally's shirt. *Whoops.*

I looked back to Nolan. His hands were now on his hips.

I tried to answer Ally quickly, to get her out of there. Nolan probably couldn't even hear a word she was saying. To him, a high school kid was leaning over my desk, after everyone else had left—knowing nothing of his presence in the doorway. It was a stupid fucking question, too. She had received a ninety-seven percent on the quiz. And she had answered the question wrong. *I think.* It's possible that I'd screwed up while grading.

I quickly explained the answer and told her that I needed to get going. Ally turned toward the door, jilted. Face flushed. She jumped back a little when she caught sight of Nolan walking into my room.

Nolan smiled down to her, said hello. She squeaked out a greeting and scurried ahead to her next class.

I might have watched her leave, and Nolan might have followed my gaze.

He hovered above my desk—all six-foot-four of him. He leaned down, right into my face and said, "Ready to lose all of your money tomorrow night?"

Seven

After a torturous day of wondering where Elsie might be, I finally called the cops. I'd put it off as long as possible. I feared
that it would still look bad. It was such a precarious situation. If
she had disappeared with everything still in our apartment, with
her pictures in my phone, and with employment at Arapahoe,
then I wouldn't have given a second thought. It was all of those
crazy factors that gave me pause.

And yes, they were crazy. I still didn't know how I was going
to explain all of that to the cops, but I was going to try.

Within an hour of reporting Elsie's disappearance, a police
cruiser arrived. Two uniformed officers stepped outside. Both
officers were young white men; the shorter of the two had a gut.

They seemed to take their time making their way up the sidewalk toward my building. It was almost like they saw me watching and wanted to build the anticipation and dread. But that wouldn't make any sense. I was an innocent man. They had no reason to suspect me of anything or to want to make me nervous. Not yet, anyway.

Within another minute, my buzzer sounded.

I let them up, and they were now standing just inside my door. I already regretted this decision, but there was no turning back now. I'd already reported her missing.

"Mr. Wallace, my name is Detective Brighton," the shorter man said. Up close, he looked a few years older than the other officer, whom he pointed to. "This is Officer Shaw. What can you tell us about your girlfriend's disappearance?" Both had notepads flipped open, pens ready.

"Well, she left and everything is gone," I said, already realizing how this was going to sound.

"So, she left you?" Brighton repeated, narrowing his eyes. "Is there any reason to suspect foul play? Any at all?"

Both officers stared me down. Why did I already feel so guilty talking to them?

This was going to be the hard part to explain. The unbelievable part. I didn't know what to do. I was glad that they apparently hadn't checked my record yet, otherwise, they would have already been more critical.

"Her phone has been disconnected. I tried calling her when I was at work, but it said that it wasn't in service."

The officers looked at each other. Shaw raised his eyebrows.

"Mr. Wallace," Detective Brighton said, quickly scribbling down a note. His eyes met mine once more. "Is it possible that she disconnected her number? Is it possible that there was *someone* she didn't want contacting her?" Shaw looked away when Brighton stressed *someone*, possibly hiding a smirk.

"I know what you're thinking, and I know how this sounds. That's why I didn't call right away. It's all so crazy."

I gauged their reactions. Nothing changed. I didn't know how much I should share. Should I explain how all of her pictures had been deleted from my phone? How her Facebook page had been deleted? They would instantly think that I was some crazy stalker, and that she was running away from me. There really wasn't any other way to look at it.

Brighton continued speaking before I could add anything else. "Actually, it doesn't sound crazy." He flipped his notepad shut. "She left and she changed her number. Maybe she finally worked up the courage."

"There's no way—" I started.

"Now, I'm not saying it's because you *stalked her* or *abused her* or anything. Maybe she just wanted a fresh start. Maybe it didn't even have anything to do with you. I'm not in a position to draw that conclusion."

Once again, Shaw hid his smirk. Brighton didn't.

"Now, unless there's anything else, we won't waste any more of *your* time," Brighton said.

I was losing them, and I was losing them quickly.

I let it all out: "Somehow, all of her pictures have been deleted from my phone. Her Facebook account was also deactivated. Literally everything that she had in this apartment is gone. I also called Arapahoe Hospital, where she told me she worked, and they had no record of her ever working there."

There, I'd laid it all out, and it sounded just as foolish as I thought it would. Maybe they would pick up on something. Maybe there was some killer out there with a similar M.O.

Brighton had flipped his notepad back open. He took down another couple of notes. Shaw did the same. Shaw glanced at his superior, waiting. Brighton finally looked up.

"Officer Shaw, what do you think?"

"I'm sorry, sir, but it doesn't sound like there's much we can do," he said, formally. "It sounds like she's gone off the grid, for whatever reason. Without any additional details, there's not much we can do to help you."

"Well said," Brighton added. "Although I wouldn't have been quite as civil." He scrutinized me, probably wondering what I could have done to make Elsie run off. "Mr. Wallace, are you *okay?*"

"What are you trying to say?" I asked, looking between the officers. "You think I'm crazy, don't you?"

Brighton slid his notepad into his pants and threw his hands up in submission. "Look, I'm not saying that. Again, I don't know what happened between you and her, but she obviously doesn't want to speak with you. For whatever reason, she took off and cut off any form of contact."

"But what about Arapahoe? Why did they say that she didn't work there?" I asked.

"Who knows?" Brighton said. "She might have worked somewhere else. She might have lied to you about her job. People do that. It doesn't raise any suspicion."

"And all of her pictures? They're all gone from my phone."

"Maybe you deleted them," Brighton said. "What else would explain that? What, do you believe that someone hacked into your phone, deleted your pictures, kidnapped your girlfriend, took everything of hers out of here, and then somehow erased her employment records at the hospital?"

I stared at him. He was right, none of it made any sense. I'd known as much. That's why I'd waited so long in contacting them. None of it added up.

"I need help," I said.

Shaw's mouth twitched. Brighton merely eyed me. I felt like he was being far too critical of me, seriously wondering what I might have done to Elsie. Maybe questioning my sanity. I continued before either one of them could confirm my self-assessment. "That's why I called this in. This isn't like Elsie. We've had a great relationship for more than a year. Just a couple weeks ago, we spent a weekend out in Breck. I *know* that she worked at Arapahoe. She always left early for her shifts. I realize this all sounds crazy, but imagine how I feel? I come home one day and everything is gone. *She's* gone. Without a trace. If I'd actually threatened her in some way, if she was truly running away from me, why would I be calling you guys?"

Brighton took in a sharp breath and let it out. "Look, I understand this is frustrating, to lose someone like this, someone you thought you knew." His tone was more sympathetic, but he still didn't believe me. "I think we've all been down this road once or twice in our lives. Okay, maybe you weren't violent. Maybe you didn't make her run for the hills, but women do leave guys for other reasons. Maybe she met someone else. Maybe you threatened her freedom. Who knows?"

I shook my head, upset with myself for thinking they could help and for subjecting myself to this. With everything I said, I made myself look more pathetic. I tried to find something to say that would make them take this seriously, but I couldn't.

"Have you talked to her family or friends?" Shaw offered, somehow humoring me.

"No. Her parents are gone," I said. "She doesn't have many friends outside of work. She talks about them some, but I've never met them."

"Well, maybe you could start there?" Shaw said.

"Look, if something else comes up, you can give us a call." Brighton gave me his card. "You have a great night, okay?"

"Sure thing," I mumbled.

And with that, they were gone. Just like Elsie. Once again, it was just me. I tried to calculate how many times I'd lied to the police. Not only this time, but also back in St. Louis.

If only there were someone else who would realize that Elsie was gone, but there seriously wasn't. I'd thought about the friends she mentioned at work, but she had mentioned only a couple of names in passing. Right now, I couldn't even remember them. And if she didn't actually work at Arapahoe Memorial, then those names were probably fake.

What about Ally or someone else on the street? Surely, they would wonder what had happened to her. Ally had always seemed to see us together. It probably wouldn't get me far though.

I'd suspected that the authorities wouldn't be able to help me. I couldn't give them anything to go on. I had a name, that was it. I had nothing to tie her to, not even a hometown.

She had mentioned growing up in the Midwest, but that was it. I was kicking myself hard for not seeing all of the signs. It reminded me of *Mr. Deeds* when the newswoman says that she's from Winchestertonfieldville, Iowa.

I was the dupe. And I wasn't even a millionaire. At least not for another eighteen years …

I stayed up all night, not doing much of anything. I finally fired up Facebook. I'd seen group pages created to help look for a missing person. That seemed like my best option, possibly my only option. Aside from waiting idly by while she was murdered by gangbangers.

I placed my laptop on my bed. The glow from the computer was the only light in the room. The sun would rise in an hour. I'd spent the entire night going over possible scenarios. That didn't help. It just increased my anxiety.

I saw that one of my friends was active. *Ally*. I cringed.

Ally had added me because she needed emergency help with

a project. I remembered seeing her desperate plea in my inbox. I think I could have replied without accepting her friend request, but even in my thirties, some of that stuff confuses me.

Or maybe I'd wanted her as a friend.

Now, I was really needing one. But she was my student, there was no way I could breach that trust. Ally was probably getting ready for her morning run.

She was so consistent, always out the door before five, even on the weekends. For a high school senior, that was almost beyond comprehension. I'm not sure if I ever woke up before five while I was in high school.

That made me think back to St. Louis, back to one of my previous encounters with law enforcement, how they had slapped the cuffs on me and said I was under arrest for my girlfriend's death. I feared history would repeat itself.

Eight

Facebook had been one of the earliest signs that something was wrong. Back when I realized that Elsie's profile had either been deleted, or that she had blocked me. I tried not to consider that the latter was a possibility. First of all, it wouldn't have made any sense. Well, again, unless she knew something. I'd like to believe that we could have moved past my history. I also would have imagined a confrontational response rather than a complete disappearing act.

All of those concerns were before I discovered the rest. That she had cleaned out our apartment, and that someone had deleted all of her pictures from my phone. That's what made me question my sanity more than the rest.

From the comfort of my couch, I stared at my Facebook newsfeed. I hadn't considered digging into the pictures of Elsie on my page until now. It's crazy to think how deep our digital imprint can go. Elsie would have to pop up in the recesses of someone's Facebook page.

Someone, somewhere … *Right?*

It'd be much easier if we had some mutual friends, but we didn't. Not one. I hadn't realized until now how crazy that was. She had talked to my sister and some of my family, but she said she felt weird about adding them on Facebook. She had always balked. She didn't have any friends in Colorado when we met, having just moved to Leadville.

I'd tried contacting a couple of my friends in the area, hoping that by some crazy miracle, they would know what had happened to her. The trouble was, I really hadn't met any friends out here either. I'd only been in Colorado for three years, and a decent portion of that time was after I'd met Elsie, and it wasn't like we went out much.

And my friends back home remembered what had happened in that crash. I wondered how many of them completely believed my story or figured I got off on a technicality. Or if they simply thought of me differently for what I'd done. I knew that some would always eye me as a threat.

That was a large part of the reason why I'd preferred to live a sheltered life with Elsie. To be homebodies. Aside from our trips out to Summit County. Even when we went snowboarding, it was usually just us. We might share the ski lift with others on our way to the top of the mountain, but those conversations were quick and informal.

I was running out of ideas.

I really needed to get into contact with some of her old friends. I needed to somehow track down her family. Nothing was adding up. I didn't even know where she'd gone to high school or where she was from.

I glanced at the bottom-right corner of my computer screen. *10:42*. I could only shake my head. How in the hell had it gotten so late? It seemed like large swaths of time kept escaping me, ever since Elsie's disappearance.

Was that some kind of by-product of emotional trauma? Losing track of time? Maybe depression, in general. I wasn't sure that I was depressed though. It had definitely sucked, but I still felt okay for the most part.

More than anything, it was confusing. A mystery that I needed to uncover. As much as I didn't want to believe it, Elsie could have been in immediate danger. Someone could have been holding her, raping her, doing God knows what else to her.

Based on all of the possibilities, her leaving me without any word would have been one of the best options, as much as it would have sucked for me.

I found myself getting sidetracked once again, jumping onto one thought, riding it out, and losing sight of my immediate task. Now, I needed to find some way to contact Elsie's past. I needed to locate her family and/or friends, at least find out where she was actually from.

I didn't know how to do this. The cops hadn't been any help. I still wasn't sure what their problem had been. They'd made me feel like I was some kind of abuser or crazy stalker. Running back through the conversation, maybe it sounded like that. Maybe I couldn't really blame them.

And then there was the question of Elsie's existence to begin with, but I'd already walked myself through that, proving to myself that Elsie was definitely real, rather than a figment of my imagination.

I got up and stretched. I twisted my back in each direction, digging my toes into the hardwood. It was my tether. I needed to be grounded to the world. Somehow, I already knew that it was going to be another long night.

Maybe it was the thought that I was crazy. I knew that I wasn't, but I'm sure that's what everyone thinks when they're deeply immersed in some twisted fabrication of reality.

My apartment was silent, far too quiet. If Elsie had been here, she would be—well, she'd be asleep right now. But if it had been a few hours earlier, in the heart of the evening, she would have had music playing—either classical or rap, rarely anything else. She'd go from Ludovico Einaudi to DaBaby and think nothing of it.

That memory wasn't going to help me. I plopped back down on the sofa, kicking my legs up in the air.

I grabbed my computer from the coffee table and pulled it close to me, pleading for an answer. Somehow, I thought that Facebook would help.

It wasn't like I could create a Facebook ad.

If only I could find a way to go viral. Maybe if I explained the entire story, how the cops wouldn't help me. Maybe that would start turning heads. Maybe people would share it. All I needed was the right person to see it.

After all, Elsie was beautiful. People would look. They'd be concerned. But, once again, I didn't have a damn picture of her.

Unbelievable.

I looked at my Facebook wall. Nothing helped. My last post was from our Breckenridge weekend. It was a lone check-in at the ski resort. We had stopped for lunch and a drink at Pioneer Crossing at the top of Peak 7.

Our bartender. What about the waiters and waitresses we'd had while going out? If I went into some of the restaurants, they would surely remember me being there with a beautiful blonde. Maybe? How much would they remember a random couple. Then again, if it was a male bartender, the odds might be higher. If only I had a picture of her.

Also, what would this prove? It would only reassure me that I wasn't completely crazy. Plus, it was Breck. There were hundreds of beautiful blonde women skiing there every day.

Pointless, really.

I went ahead and did something that would end up being both incredibly positive and negative. I posted a Facebook plea. Maybe I should have thought it through a little more, but I was so tired and stressed. I wasn't exactly in my optimal, prime state of mind.

I'd barely considered how people—even those close to me—would react. The situation was too similar to what had happened before. The loss and the pain. People suspecting that I had been responsible. Or even if I hadn't been directly responsible, that I was still a horrible man.

Oh well. I went ahead and typed out my message. I needed to do something to try to bring Elsie home.

I hate to make this public, but I feel like I have no other choice. As some of you know, I'm dating a woman named Elsie Morton. A couple of days ago, she vanished from our apartment.

I first knew something was wrong when I tried calling her earlier in the day, but her phone had been disconnected. When I arrived home after work, all of her belongings had been removed. Her clothes, her toothbrush, everything. I notified the cops, but they think that she just ran away and changed her phone number and deleted Facebook because she is trying to avoid me. They won't do anything for me, so I'm hoping that someone else can help me.

I'm not sure what else can be done ... Elsie would not leave without saying anything. We had a great relationship. Most of you know me. You know that she wouldn't need to run from me. Please, someone, anyone. If you know anything about where she might be, please send me a message. You may also feel free to share this post.

Thank you.

I didn't even review it before pressing enter. I knew that it probably sounded desperate and pleading. I could sense people rolling their eyes and saying, "Man, just let her go." That was also on the nicer end of the responses. I feared there were some who thought I was dangerous.

MATT RIEDLE

I didn't even wait around to see if anyone responded right away. If there were messages, I'd see them later. Instead, I closed the computer, slamming it a little too hard. Hopefully, I didn't break anything. I didn't even check.

I got up from the couch and went to my bedroom, fighting back tears. I'm not even sure what the tears were from … loss, frustration, anger, fatigue? Maybe all of the above.

Nine

Trying to work in the middle of the firestorm was becoming increasingly difficult, especially in light of posting the Facebook plea. Word gets around quickly, and now everyone knew that something was up. The students and faculty had organized into four factions: I was either an innocent victim, I'd gone insane and possibly butchered Elsie, or that the reality was somewhere in the middle—that I'd committed some egregious act that forced her to leave, she had retaliated, and we were both at fault. It also felt like a few others doubted that Elsie even existed.

Before walking into class, I overheard the end of a conversation between Ally and Michelle. They were talking near the back of the room, so I hung out just outside the door before entering, hoping to get some idea of what was waiting for me inside. *Creeping.*

"I think it's like *Gone Girl,*" Ally said. "She's just a psychotic bitch. I bet Mark didn't really do anything wrong. He might not have loved her as much, but that's what happens in a relationship. Especially when you get older."

"It's 'Mark' now?" Michelle asked critically.

"Shut up," Ally shot back, smirking.

Michelle continued. "Well, if he's dating a crazy bitch, then he kind of had this coming, didn't he? They're probably both messed up. Like attracts like."

"No, not Mark. He's so ..." Ally began, in a melodic tone.

Michelle leaned in closer. "Did you fuck him?"

Several wide-eyed students turned toward her.

I almost choked. And then I was busted.

"Mr. Wallace?"

I spun around. Darius Hayes stood next to a line of lockers with a book in hand. We were about eye-to-eye.

"Oh, Darius." I tried to compose myself. "Are you psyched to learn about the American Revolution today?"

His eyes shot wide. "Super psyched." He entered the room ahead of me. The girls had stopped talking, at least audibly.

As I walked past their desks, I tried not to make eye contact. Lately, I was hesitant to lock eyes with many of my students, fearful of what I would see.

From my desk, a bank of windows sat to my right. When all else failed, I looked outside at the trees.

When I glanced outside, I thought I saw someone duck behind a large tree, framed by a graying sky. I continued to look for a few seconds, waiting for someone to peek around.

A nervous laugh came from my left. I turned back to face the class. Several students shifted in their seats. Not sure what my expression was, but it couldn't have been comforting.

Without even intending to, I looked directly at Ally. She blushed and looked down. Michelle looked from Ally to me, back to Ally. Michelle raised her eyebrows.

"Okay, class, uh," I said, looking back outside. Flurries had just started to fall. There was no sign of anyone on the front lawn of the school. Had I imagined it?

I turned back. Twenty-four pairs of eyes looked in three directions. Some down, some at me, some outside. It wouldn't have surprised me if their looks corresponded with how they felt about me, about Elsie's disappearance, aligned along those same three (or four) factions.

I was able to gain my footing and make it through the class. Aside from the one glance at Ally, I'd kept my eyes from wandering back to her. To anyone.

As the class was filing out—bumping against desks, shouting over one another, I looked back outside.

And there she was ... *Elsie*.

She was standing next to the tree, looking back at me. A blank expression on her face. That look. Indecipherable. Often passed from one human to another. It could have meant anything from "You're going to die tonight" to "I miss you."

I turned my head, smiled slightly. I raised my hand to wave, but she didn't respond in any perceptible way.

And then she vanished from my life.

Again.

Or had she even been there?

I'd definitely imagined it. I was losing control over everything, my life and my mind.

Ten

I had a free period after watching Elsie vanish behind the tree. After she disappeared, I galloped down the hallway, eliciting stares from many of the students. Some stopped to watch, others pretended not to see anything. I also caught a few glances from my coworkers.

Those weren't good. They knew I was losing my mind, that I was endangering the students' focus and wellbeing.

Even before setting foot on the frozen ground, now dusted with snow, I knew that she was long gone.

I looked regardless.

I jogged toward the tree where I'd seen her, hands in my coat pockets. "Elsie?" I called out, trying not to be too loud. Thankfully, it was cold and all of the windows were closed.

It didn't look like anyone had left footprints around the tree. If she had been here, she surely would have left a trace. It hadn't snowed enough to cover her tracks.

I looked back at where I'd walked … Footprints.

They weren't deep, as there wasn't enough snow, but I had clearly left footprints. Elsie was a ghost.

"Elsie?" I called out again, this time louder. My breath exploded into the frigid air. For maybe a minute—maybe longer, I could do nothing but stare at my breath.

I was running out of ideas. Elsie had been here, outside my classroom. I knew it. But she wasn't here. She wasn't anywhere. I hadn't seen her in days. And yet, I felt her presence everywhere. Behind the tree, inside of me. It was like she had never left, but also like she had never been in my life.

The total absence of her belongings in my apartment may have troubled me most. I couldn't even find any hair pins when I'd vacuumed the day before.

That's unexplainable. Those things usually remain for months after a woman has moved out.

My ears and nose ached from the cold. The snow whipped around me; the wind had picked up. I took a deep breath and exhaled. Fool's errand. It was time to get back inside. I'd try to do a little grading during my next class.

I turned back toward the school. The windows were lined with faces staring back at me. How long had they been watching?

From outside, I couldn't tell what they were saying, but I knew it was likely at my expense.

I raised my eyebrows slightly, dropped my head, and jogged back to the front doors of the school. When I glanced up, the inquisitive faces were gone. The students—and teachers—were back in their seats, or at least away from the windows.

Weird.

When I reached the door, the bell rang. I'd somehow been outside in the cold for nearly fifty minutes.

When I returned home that night, I broke down. I sat on the edge of a living room chair, cradling my head in my hands. The apartment was too quiet. It had been deadly still since she left.

I wasn't sure how an apartment could so quickly transform from a lover's escape to a constant reminder of what had been lost. When she was here, there was so much life, not just in the apartment, but also within me.

Yeah, okay, that was a little melodramatic. Yet I desperately needed answers.

Eleven

The night finally came for the big poker game. A guy can't let a little pissing and moaning break tradition. It was a familiar phrase … I knew I'd heard it somewhere before. Maybe from *Wedding Crashers?*

It was obviously more than just a little pissing and moaning. Elsie was still missing, and I had no idea what had happened. I was still getting the runaround from authorities, and my Facebook plea had actually been deleted for violating community standards. Not sure how or why. I felt like it had been gaining traction. It had even generated a few leads, even though they were from total nutjobs. I was tempted to write another post, just to see what would happen.

But yeah, I was losing my focus again.

The poker game. That was all that mattered tonight.

I hadn't planned on canceling the poker game, but a couple of guys had called to cancel. I didn't press them for an excuse, but their reasoning seemed a little weak. I didn't really care. There would be at least five of us. That's all we really needed.

On the way home, I stopped by a gas station to grab a couple thirty-packs of Miller Lite. If someone wanted some craft beer, they'd have to bring it. The Miller brewery actually wasn't too far away from where I lived, about thirty minutes.

I thought back to going to the brewery tours a couple times with Elsie. It was an awesome tour. They gave you plenty of free samples; that was about all I'd usually limit myself to.

I went to the counter with a thirty-pack in each hand. As I approached the counter, I thought I felt someone looking at me from the parking lot. There was a defined presence. I looked over, but I didn't see anyone. By that time, they had surely moved. I couldn't help but wonder if Elsie was still keeping an eye on me. Or maybe it had been someone else?

"$36.18," the cashier repeated. I'd barely registered him the first time.

"Sorry," I said, still looking outside through the front windows. "I was a little distracted."

"It's all good," the guy said. "Good luck with that."

I laughed a little, and then I drove back to my place.

I set up the fancy card table in the middle of our living area. I moved the couch over to the side to give us a little more room.

Vice Principal Nolan brought over the community chips that we always used. Kyle Bellamy showed up, along with a football coach and a math teacher.

We played five-card draw. We all bought in for two hundred dollars each. Yeah, it was a serious poker game—at least for a group of teachers. It probably wasn't the best thing to be doing on a school night, but most of the guys were usually too busy on the weekends.

Thursday night drinking sent me back to the college days. As did playing poker with a few other guys. I didn't know if that was going to be a good thing ...

An hour later, we were in the middle of the game. Nobody had really gained an advantage yet.

"Call," I said, carefully eying my cards.

"Are you sure you want to do that?" Kyle asked.

"What you got, big boy?" I asked, holding eye contact.

Kyle threw down a pair of jacks, visibly feeling good about his chances.

I smirked, dropping three queens onto the table.

I made a move for the pot, but then Kyle put down three sevens. "Full house," he said. "You thought you had me, didn't you, Marky Mark?"

That made me think back to Elsie again. She'd occasionally text me while I was out, but it was usually just to see how much fun I was having. Her messages were usually brief and understanding. She was cool about things like that. I guess she realized that I didn't go out too often.

The night was a nice release. Those who showed up didn't seem to treat me any differently.

After a couple of beers, I decided to prod Kyle a little. Maybe I could learn more about the mysterious music teacher.

"So where were you at before you came out here?" I asked.

"I was in Dallas … Dallas, Texas." Kyle said, giving his best Texan voice.

"So, what, you're like this traveling music teacher or what?"

Kyle chuckled. "Man, have you seen our backyard? How could someone not live out here?"

He had a point.

"Where'd you come from, St. Louis?" Kyle asked, eyes narrowing on me. He knew. But I couldn't be surprised by this. Although I hadn't included my prior information in the school directory (for fear of students looking at me differently), it was easy information to obtain. All anyone had to do was search for me on Google. It would have been hard for me to hide that unless I changed my name.

"That's right," I said, taking a drink. "Grew up in Edwardsville, Illinois. It's on the Illinois-side of St. Louis. I moved to St. Louis after college—Soulard."

Kyle raised his eyebrows and shook his head. "Well, those towns don't mean anything to me, but I do know St. Louis. Glad to be out here, aren't you, Marky Mark?"

"I am," I said.

"And we are glad to have him," Nolan said, before raising the bet. I folded.

Kyle raised, and Nolan had to go all-in. Kyle took him out with trip-sevens. Nolan had bluffed with a pair of sixes.

"Damn," Nolan said. "Glad I get paid tomorrow. I'm going to grab an Uber. I really don't want to get a D.U.I. on a school night. Might look bad to the student body."

I tensed. That comment couldn't have been intentional, but I hadn't been ready for it. It took me back for a split-second.

"Sounds good," I said, hoping that nobody caught my initial reaction. I thought Bellamy had eyed me.

"I'll wait outside and get some fresh air. Take care, guys," Nolan said, and then he was off.

Not long after, Kyle and I took the other two guys out.

"It's just you and me, cowboy," I said.

Kyle had a slight chip advantage, but I was hungry. I needed to win something. I needed something to go right for me. I thought that I could take him. Maybe in more ways than one.

"What was that about the other day—in the hallway?" I asked, now that I had some liquid courage. "When you said it would be understandable to cancel … given the circumstances."

"Marky Mark," Kyle said. "You're not still thinking about that, are you?"

Actually, I was. Granted, I'd thought about Elsie much more, but I couldn't shake how Kyle had known.

"I just don't know how you knew about Elsie," I said. "I hadn't told anyone yet. I'd only called the hospital."

"What?" he asked, one eyebrow cocked. "I meant since I knew I was going to take all your money, just like I always do."

He laughed, but I noticed a catch, like he was hiding something. Or maybe I was just losing my mind.

Regardless, I backed off, and we resumed our game.

We went back and forth for a little while. During the back and forth, we added a few more beers. I probably already drank way too much. By this time, the music was also loud.

It was nearly four when I realized that Kyle was passed out on the floor. I honestly wasn't sure who won or if we had finished the game. I was already feeling pretty good, but I wasn't ready to call it a night.

I should have also passed out, but instead, I cracked open another beer. I'd lost track of how many I'd had—at least a twelve-pack. I went ahead and grabbed one *for the road* before heading back to my room. My plan was to sit in my room and listen to music. Shut out the world.

Drinking with the guys always made me nostalgic for my college days. So naturally, I tended to gravitate toward the songs that reminded me of college parties. That wonderful music of the early-to-mid 2000s, dashed with the classic rock hits of the 70s and 80s. I jumped from 50 Cent to Journey, back to Nelly. Before I knew it, I had a few empties in front of me. At some point, I must have marched to the kitchen for more.

It was getting closer to sunrise. Something was keeping me from passing out, and I knew what it was. Admitting it to myself made me feel a little sick. I knew it wasn't a good idea.

From behind the curtains, I peeked outside. It wasn't quite twilight, but it was getting close. The birds chirped, generally the first signs of the world coming to life. Soon, the rising sun would torch the sky.

Before the abrupt change in my life, it would have been a great morning for a run. Although we were still in the depths of winter, Chinook winds had moved in overnight, resulting in a mild morning.

A run in my condition might kill me. Maybe I would just step outside to get some air. The warmer air would be refreshing after the recent cold spell. The truth was that any fresh air would be good for my drunk ass. Hot, frigid, whatever.

I polished off another beer. I promised myself that it would be my last. My collection of cans was up to six. Add that to what I'd drunk before, and yeah, it was quite an accomplishment.

Now, I was more concerned with seeing the other woman in my life. One who hadn't completely disappeared.

Twelve

She would be outside any minute. Not Elsie, but Ally. My drunkenness had me trying to rationalize things. She was eighteen, an adult. If I wasn't her teacher, things could have easily been different.

But still, I just wanted to see her.

It didn't help that Elsie wasn't here. Sure, I'd thought of Ally before, but I'd never seriously considered following through.

Yes, I'd talked to her on Messenger, and that's what I was afraid that Elsie had discovered. If she hadn't had the right context, maybe that is what prompted her to take off. But it was all harmless. Maybe some innocent flirting.

Look, but don't touch. Forbidden fruit.

Once again, Elsie wasn't here. She'd left me alone. Abruptly. If she wouldn't have left, I definitely wouldn't be considering anything. Then again, I didn't know for sure what had happened. Maybe Elsie really was innocent in this. Maybe she had been the target of some crazy operation.

I wasn't dissuaded, and the alcohol wasn't helping my reasoning capabilities.

And I'd probably be fired soon, anyway, so what the hell?

As if on cue, Ally emerged from her house with her dog. She wore those black leggings that left little to the imagination.

Within a minute, I had emerged on the sidewalk. Ally must have already stretched inside because she was already halfway down our block. *Damn.* Oh well, it was almost better this way. It might not look like I'd watched her from the window and come outside right after she had.

And it was a mild morning. A soft breeze rustled the leaves above my head. I tried to look, but my head started to spin. Maybe I had just turned my head too quickly. I reoriented myself and looked back down the block, toward where Ally had taken off. I didn't see her. Maybe she had turned the corner.

I didn't really want to chase after her. Instead, I crossed the street and started around the block in the opposite direction. That way, it might not look so creepy if I ran into her. I was probably overthinking it, anyway. Hell, I knew I was overthinking it. She wouldn't care if I ran into her. She'd probably welcome it.

What was I hoping for here? That we would run into each

other, flirt, and I'd take her back upstairs while her mom fixed her breakfast. Come to think of it, I'm not sure I'd ever seen her mom or dad. They were probably off working in God knows what city, leaving her to fend for herself. She seemed like she might have been the type.

I jogged for a while, playing out possible scenarios, honestly not thinking much about Elsie at the time.

And then it happened.

"Mark!" Ally shrieked. "What are you doing out here?"

I nearly fell over. My head had been in space. I was also working on fighting through the alcohol. "Hey, Ally," I finally managed to say. She slowed, I slowed, and then we both stopped. "I thought I'd get a run in this morning."

"Did you even sleep?" She grinned. "It looked like you had quite the party last night. I was jealous."

Was she watching me?

"Just a little poker game, nothing too crazy."

"Whatever." She laughed. "You can be honest with me. Besides, Mr. Bellamy posted on TikTok last night."

I didn't fail to realize that she had called him Mr. Bellamy instead of Kyle, but she had no problem calling me Mark.

"He what?" I asked, indignant.

She threw her head back, laughing. I caught myself eyeing her neck, picturing pressing my lips in the crease between her neck and shoulder.

She continued. "Don't worry, you were super cute." She bit her lip, batting her eyebrows. "You're brave, Mark. I know it must be *so hard* after Elsie left you." Her eyes shot to just below my waist.

Ally knew she had me.

She knew that I was drunk and vulnerable. If she ever wanted to shoot her shot, this was the time. But no, I couldn't do it. No way. Not if I ever had any dream of teaching again.

I felt bad that my thoughts went immediately to my career, not to Elsie. Not simply wanting to remain faithful. Then again, I didn't know where Elsie was …

How in the hell could Elsie just leave me?

I swallowed.

I needed to keep this from escalating any further. "Shouldn't you be getting ready for school?"

"Shouldn't you?" she echoed, reaching toward me, without hesitation. She was insanely confident. She knew exactly what she wanted and was going for it.

"Ally!" I spun away, shooting my eyes wide. "What are you doing? Not out here."

"But somewhere?" she said, fixated. "Come over to my place. I'll leave the door unlocked. Catch me coming out of the shower." She lowered her voice. "I'll be nice and wet."

"What about your parents?" I asked, realizing that I hadn't even rejected her sultry proposal.

She looked at a passing car, her grin disappearing for a quick second. "They're both away. It's just me for a while."

"I can't. Elsie is—"

"Pussy," she said, giving me a playful shove, and then she

took off, jogging past me. "If you change your mind, you know where to find me."

It was one thing to think about this happening, but there was no way that I could do it. Not with Elsie missing.

I went home.

Thirteen

I barely made it to work that morning. Ally didn't make it to school. Thankfully. I'd turned her down. I didn't want to face her. I maintained the façade of holding it together while most of the students and co-workers looked at me like I was a ruthless, psychotic killer.

Or maybe they just thought I was crazy, especially after posting the story on Facebook. Crazy or maybe pathetic. I hated how it sounded, like I was just caught up on someone who obviously didn't want anything to do with me—that I was some kind of an obsessed creeper.

I dealt with the looks though. I had to keep working, as

long as they'd let me. It gave me a sense of normalcy. During some of my class periods—while engaged in a lecture, I'd even forget that Elsie was gone.

Ally, too.

Similar to the day after Elsie left (was taken, or whatever), I was running late to a class. And just like that day, so was the Texan, Kyle Bellamy.

"Late again? Man, this is *so* unlike you," he chimed. "I guess that's what happens though, isn't it? When your life comes crashing down around you?"

I raised an eyebrow, unsure of how to respond. In that moment, I honestly wanted to clock him, to knock that pompous, shit-eating grin off of his face.

Instead, I responded as responsibly as I could manage. "It's been tough. I had trouble sleeping again."

"Oh, yeah?" he asked, grinning. "How are your students? How's Ally?"

"What the fuck did you say?" I asked, forgetting that I was in a high school and needed to censor myself.

"Language, language," Kyle said, casting faux-worried glances in each direction. "Marky, Mark, what has gotten into you lately? You're usually so mild mannered."

I stared him down, but he continued to smile, unnerved. He knew that I couldn't do anything, not here, not anywhere.

He grasped my shoulder and shook me. "I'll see you around. Tell the Funky Bunch that I said hey."

It actually took me a second to process *Marky Mark and the*

Funky Bunch. My mind wasn't quite at optimal performance. I was getting tired of these run-ins with Kyle, but there wasn't much I could do about it.

Why had he asked about Ally? What did he know? And *how* could he have known? It reminded me of the comment he had made right after Elsie had disappeared. Bellamy knew more than anyone else should have.

But thinking back to Ally ... He had come over to play poker that night, but he had passed out well before I ran into Ally. Ally had mentioned that he had posted a TikTok video that night. That got me wondering, *Had Ally posted something about me? A video?* Maybe Kyle had seen it.

I didn't think Ally would be so foolish. If she posted a Tik-Tok featuring me, I would be hearing from more than Kyle. He would be the least of my concerns. Actually, Kyle *was* the least of my concerns, but they were all starting to pile up.

I was struggling enough with my hangover and thinking about what might have happened to my girlfriend.

My mysterious girlfriend.

There were large swaths of Elsie's past that I didn't know. She had told me about her childhood and some stories from high school. She also told me about the vacations her family used to take—she had visited Colorado a few times, and she had also been to London.

But whenever I'd ask her about any specifics after high school, she'd become withdrawn. Physically, she'd inch away from me, but emotionally, that inch may as well have been a mile. She'd generally responded by saying, "I'll just bore you. You don't want to hear about that." But then she would go somewhere in her head, thinking back to whatever it was that she didn't want to share.

I desperately wanted to pull her back. To know that some-one close to you is hiding something, it can be difficult. I'd wanted to respect her privacy, but I also wanted to somehow help her.

She had mentioned one trip to west Texas and New Mexico. I wasn't sure she meant to, but one time I suggested that we go down to Taos to snowboard. I thought the area seemed cool and it could be a nice escape for us. She said that she had passed through the area a few years ago.

I'd asked her about more details, but once again, she didn't give me much. I just wish she could have been a little more open with me. Such a fine line between letting someone's past be their past and knowing more to become closer. Something was defi-nitely bothering her.

If I knew, maybe I'd be able to resolve it. Then again, some secrets are probably better left unsaid. She probably feared that I'd look at her differently, and hell, maybe I would have. It's hard to say. And although she became distant whenever it came up, those instances were few and far between. Most of the time, we were close. So, I'd let it go.

Well, until she would wake me up with her violent night-mares. I'd taken several elbows to the head, as well as getting hair-whipped across the face. Yes, she had spun so quickly that her hair had to be flying one hundred miles per hour when it slapped into me.

After waking, she would occasionally turn to me, wide-eyed, and say something along the lines of, "They got me."

In a daze, I'd ask, "Who?" but then she'd just lie down and go back to sleep. By the time morning came, she'd seldom be able to remember anything about the dreams. Or maybe she just didn't want me to know what they were about.

So many secrets.

Maybe I should have asked her more. Maybe I should have persisted. Could I have saved her? Maybe we could have avoided … *this.* Whatever *this* was. Disappearance, vanishing, kidnapping, abandonment. Whatever.

I sighed at the last thought. Nah, Elsie wouldn't leave me.

Then again, I entertained the thought that maybe she didn't need to be saved. I kept thinking that something horrible might have happened to her and that she didn't want to bring up her past because she was a victim, but maybe I was completely mistaken. Maybe I had underestimated her.

It was time to figure this out. Beyond time, really. I'd had nothing to go on for several days. Staying in my head wasn't going to do anything for me.

It would only drive me crazy.

Fourteen

The next day sucked. Once again, Ally didn't show up to school. I hadn't even seen her jogging the last two mornings. I wasn't sure what had happened to her. Maybe she felt guilty and awkward about our little rendezvous. Maybe she needed some time to pull herself back together. Or maybe she was sick. There were many explanations.

After my seventh hour class ended—the same one with Ally, Vice Principal Nolan assumed his same spot in the doorway as the day that Ally had asked questions about her quiz.

He had nearly the same expression, but this time, I didn't think he was going to joke about poker night. This time, he didn't even walk into my room. He barely even looked at me.

"Thanks for giving me your money the other night," I said, trying to lighten the mood.

"Look, Mark, I hate to be so blunt here, but I need you to follow me to my office. I don't want to be the guy to do this … I've never had a problem with you, but … something has recently been brought to our attention."

I heard him, but I didn't respond. I was in a daze. I stared at my gradebook, covered on one side by homework that the class had just turned in. Nothing of major importance. Not really. None of it was comparatively important.

Nolan continued, "Mr. Wallace? Mark?"

I looked up. His eyes narrowed.

"I'd ask that you follow me to my office."

I didn't even ask what it was about, not sure I even wanted to know. Instead, I exhaled loudly, pushed my chair back—into the wall, and stood.

"All right," I said. "Let's go."

I followed him outside my room, down the hall, to his office. During the march, I didn't think about much, nothing other than the melodic sound of my shoes slapping against the tile. Exhaustion had become my default. I seldom remembered sleeping. Even when I thought that I'd enjoyed a full night of sleep, I'd wake up more tired than I'd been the night before.

When I entered Nolan's office, I realized that this was a *party*. Several others were in the room. Principal Tina Worthington, the other assistant, Julius Nicks, and the Superintendent, Reese Vance. They all offered lifeless greetings.

I slumped down in a chair, feeling like I was a student who was about to be expelled … or perhaps a teacher who was about to be fired.

"Let's get started. Please be seated." Superintendent Vance took charge, taking a seat behind Nolan's desk. Everyone else formed an arc extending outward from the desk. I was in the middle, slumped over. Nolan was to my immediate right, Nicks to my left. I think Worthington was somewhere.

Behind the desk was a small window, looking out across the front of the school. I could see the tree where Elsie had appeared. Except now it had a few inches of snow blasted around its base. The sunshine made the snow sparkle, a stark contrast to the mood inside Nolan's office.

"Mr. Wallace, we have recently received a disturbing accusation." She paused. I shifted my gaze from the window to her. She continued. "It is an accusation involving sexual activity with one of your students."

"What?" I blinked. My chest warmed. Focus narrowed. I feigned shock, but it wasn't like I didn't know what they were talking about.

"We take this type of accusation seriously. Until we have time to investigate, we have no choice—"

"Anyone can make an accusation," I shot back. "That doesn't mean that I'm guilty of having sex with one of my students."

"We haven't accused you of such," Principal Worthington said, sternly.

I mindlessly scratched the (rapidly-accruing) stubble on my chin, closing my eyes for an extended second. They seemed to be waiting for a response. I glanced back at Vance. Her black hair fell to her shoulders—curtains of death. I'd never thought of her that way until today.

"I'm no expert on criminal law, but it sure feels like I am being accused. If I wasn't being accused, I wouldn't be here."

Nobody said anything.

Nolan and Worthington exchanged glances. Vance continued to look at me. I realized that the scene outside the window looked much more inviting than it really was. Blue sky, bright sun, sparkling snow … but it was still frigid.

"Mr. Wallace," Vance said. "While these claims are investigated, we will put you on paid leave. I hope you understand that we do this to protect the students from distraction." She paused, possibly waiting for me to lash out, but I didn't have it in me. I simply stared back. She continued. "Considering other, extenuating circumstances, the time off might serve you well."

"Extenuating circumstances? You mean, like my missing girlfriend?"

"Yes." Vance nodded. "That's exactly what I mean."

I looked back at the tree. Elsie wasn't there. Vance finally followed my gaze, but she quickly turned back. Apparently, she wasn't impressed with the view.

"This is only temporary," Worthington said. "Once this is all cleared up, we will gladly welcome you back."

I might have smiled at her. I'd always liked Tina.

"Okay," I said. "If this is how it has to be, then it sounds like I don't have a choice." I rose from my chair, suddenly ready to get far away from the school. Far away from everything would be ideal. I wondered if Ally had turned me in.

Or maybe Kyle?

Nolan and Nicks stood next to me, looking like they were acting as emergency bodyguards for Vance—just in case I tried to lunge across her desk.

Instead, I brushed around Nolan and left the room. The hallway was empty, void of students. The hallways were almost eerie between classes. How quickly they could transform from vibrant population centers to abandoned alleys.

If only I could get to my classroom, collect my things, and exit the school without running into anyone.

But my current luck wouldn't allow that.

I made it to my classroom without incident, grateful that I hadn't dropped off anything in the teacher's lounge. I wasn't even sure how long it had been since I'd been in the lounge. If they didn't want to see me, then I didn't want to see them.

After leaving Nolan's office, I considered how the administrators viewed the situation. Worthington seemed to defend me, was almost warm during the meeting. Nicks didn't say much, probably completely undecided. As for Vance and Nolan? Hell, it's not like it really mattered what they thought. I needed to conserve my critical thinking for relevant issues.

I glanced at the clock. I'd wasted some time in thought, but I still had fifteen minutes to make my great escape. Ample time.

If I wasn't out by then, Vance might call for security to escort me off the grounds.

Yeah, Vance was against me.

I hadn't even thought of who I was alleged to have *assaulted.* Didn't really need to. I knew it was Ally. I doubted that she turned me in though. Probably someone who had seen us, or heard us … talking.

Her desk was empty now, but I looked, then exhaled. I glanced outside at the tree. As expected, I didn't see anything. But I knew Elsie had been there. That haunting, blank expression on her face.

With ten minutes remaining before the bell, I collected my coat, computer, briefcase, and a few other random items, including the pencil holder that Elsie had given me.

When I reached the door, I gave the room one last look. I didn't think I'd be back for a while, if ever. It was only my third year in the classroom, but I felt like I'd been a resident much longer. It was difficult to turn away and leave.

Seven minutes left.

I finally turned away from my room, taking another step in my great escape. I shuffled through the quiet hallways, trying not to glance inside the other rooms as I passed. It was easier said than done.

Terrance Mullins, math teacher, caught my eye as I passed. He immediately looked away. A junior girl did the same thing. A senior gave me a conciliatory smile before flipping her hair out of her face.

I wonder how many of them already knew. The other teachers surely wouldn't have said anything to the students, but all it takes is one person overhearing a conversation. Or, if whoever made the complaint told others ... then it would spread like wildfire. High school students would eat that shit up.

Just before I reached the door, I ran into someone I really didn't want to see ... and didn't want to be seen with.

There wasn't any avoiding her. She came down the steps and stood between me and the door to the parking lot.

She had been looking down as she descended the stairs. When she hit the first floor, she looked up, and instantly locked eyes with me. She might have jumped a little.

"Ally," I said, giving her a slight nod.

"Mark," she said. "Sorry, Mr. Wallace." She smiled slyly. "Is everything okay? Your girlfriend?"

"Great," I said, looking away from her eyes, ignoring her piercing, knowing questions. "Enjoy the rest of your day."

"I just came to pick up some things. I haven't been feeling like myself lately." And then she leaned up to my ear and whispered, "Not since you grabbed my hips ..." Her breath became throatier. "And pushed yourself deep inside me."

My eyes shot wide. "I did not," I said, blood pulsing, but careful not to raise my voice too loudly.

Ally broke away from me, but only slightly. She looked up at me, grinning, expectant.

My urge was to push her away from me, but that would surely result in a quick arrest.

Instead, I quickly shuffled around Ally, I and was out the door, dispatched into the cold.

Exiled.

While driving back to my apartment, I sensed that I was being followed—trailed through the streets of suburban Denver.

Fifteen

Back in the comfort of my apartment, I thought about what had happened. It always happens so quickly, those life-altering events. Suspended? No way. But I knew exactly why. I wasn't sure why Ally would have turned me in though. Or maybe it was Kyle Bellamy.

Hell, it wasn't like it really mattered anymore. With everything going on, with my work suffering, I'd probably end up being fired.

I thought back to that night in St. Louis when that all unraveled. Riley. The drinks. The blood. Sitting in the jail cell.

There was no point thinking about that. It was history. I'd done my best to move forward with my life. I'd met Elsie.

We had dated for more than a year.

If I hadn't been so headstrong about leaving everything behind, maybe I would have been more critical about Elsie's nonexistent past. Instead, I'd been so eager for a sense of normalcy. I just wanted to put the pieces back together and build a life for myself.

Picking back up with my career had been easy enough, especially once the charges had been dropped. Otherwise, if I'd been convicted or pled guilty to any of the charges, I probably wouldn't have been able to teach again.

I'd hoped that as long as I could cling to my career during this onslaught, that I'd be okay.

But now I didn't have anything.

Numerous calls, texts, and messages had come through since Elsie's disappearance—since I had posted on Facebook, anyway. Most were easily screened. One example was a guy who claimed that Elsie had appeared to him in a dream, telling him that the mothership was coming back into the Earth's orbit and everyone worthy of saving would be led by Elsie to Mount Whitney in California.

But one was different. Someone by the name of Horace Qualls. He must have actually known Elsie because he knew she was from Chicago—he'd even given me the name of a high school. It was intriguing enough. I needed to check it out.

We had arranged to meet at Starbucks. Well, *he* had offered to meet at Starbucks. I laughed a little when he offered, mentally tallying up how much business they had lost since Elsie's disappearance. But for all I knew, she was keeping up her latte habit. She would probably die if she stopped now.

I sat at a table for two near the back door. I hadn't ordered anything. Hopefully, they wouldn't have me arrested for loitering. I naturally thought of my arrest back in St. Louis.

For homicide.

It had been a warm spring day, maybe a little muggy. It was a nice afternoon though. It was one of those first days where people went out for patio dinners.

When I recount the memory, it usually skips ahead to leaving my apartment and hearing the storm approach. A light rain began to fall.

I pushed it aside, just like every other time the memory threatened to consume me. I needed to focus on Elsie and trying to bring her back to me.

Elsie, not Riley. Focus.

Back in the present—at Starbucks, it was early evening, so the tables were primarily occupied by students studying.

I realized that I'd made the mistake of not asking Horace what he would be wearing. I'd have to go by his Facebook picture, but I wasn't sure if I'd recognize him in a crowd.

After entering, I'd glanced around the sitting area, but nobody stuck out. I ordered a hot mocha and then sat down to wait. Nobody had joined me by the time my name was called.

I grabbed my drink and sat back down, mindlessly thumbing

through a newspaper left on the table. An article about an up-coming winter storm caught my eye. They were forecasting a huge dump for the ski resorts.

It was a mental escape. I was just thinking about how awe-some it would be to head out there when a large shadow blocked the light and brought me back to reality, made me remember why I was here.

"Mark?" the man asked, barely above a whisper, like he didn't want anyone to hear. He cast furtive glances around him, making sure that he was clear.

"Horace?" I asked, matching his volume.

He nodded. I stood and we shook hands. I motioned for him to sit down, and he took a seat opposite, once again looking behind him before sitting.

His Facebook picture was a bit misleading. He looked sev-eral years older now, but he was dapper. He was dressed in a noticeably nice suit and carried a briefcase.

"How do you know Elsie?" I said, cutting to the chase.

He looked around once again. "I can't stay long. I think someone has been following me." He delicately slung his brief-case onto the table, unzipping the large compartment.

"Following you? Who?" I demanded. "Elsie?"

He didn't say anything. Instead, he pulled out a hardcover book and met my eyes.

"What is that?" I asked. "Who is following you?"

"I'm not sure who, but I'm sure it has something to do with Sydney," he said.

"Sydney?" I asked. "Who?"

"Here." He handed me the book and stood to leave. "You'll find what you're looking for. I need to go."

"Wait," I said, pleading with him to stay, but he had already left and the door had shut behind him.

I finally looked at the book he had left. It was an old high school yearbook. I didn't know how in the hell this was supposed to help me, but I'd quickly find out.

Naturally, I flipped through the classes, searching the M's for Elsie Morton. *Nothing.* And then I thought back to what Horace said—about Sydney. But before looking, I needed to leave Starbucks, get home. Maybe it was only because of Horace, but I definitely felt like I was being watched.

Sixteen

The six men entered the room, greeting each other with a nod and a handshake before sitting. They were all solemn, as there was serious business to attend to this afternoon.

They met in a Chicago high-rise, overlooking a glittering Lake Michigan. A large window stretched the length of the room, dominated by an oval conference table. The men took their seats, paying no attention to the expansive view.

They spent the first thirty minutes going over pressing issues in their business, about the shipment of certain goods and the procurement of funds. Their industry did well. They definitely had their connections.

On the subject of money, one of the men informed the others that he needed to make a call to ensure receipt. He also needed an update on an issue that had plagued their organization for more than a decade.

"*Privyet,*" he said, after the call had been answered, a familiar greeting. "Have you received the money?" he asked.

The other men looked on; this stage was more of a formality as they assumed that the money had already been received.

"Very well," he said, confirming their thoughts. His accent was thick. He had spoken English for many years, but it still came out sharp and halting.

"Also, do you have any news to share with us?"

The voice on the other end was catching. He knew this. But why, he did not know. What purpose could there be to hide the truth? It made him suspicious, but maybe he was on edge. Maybe he was furious about waiting so long to bring his son justice.

For now, he wouldn't question. If the suspicion deepened, he would have to take action.

Instead, he wrapped up their call.

"*Paka paka,* little rabbit," he said, smiling slightly. It was the closest thing to emotion that he would show in the presence of his men. They didn't think any less of him. They knew what he had lost, and they were all just as eager to find the person responsible.

The man ended the call and returned his focus to the men.

"The money has been received. Now, let us continue with our business."

Seventeen

From the perceived safety of my bedroom, I finally began my search for Sydney. I honestly didn't know if I'd find Elsie or if it would be someone completely different. Maybe Horace had her confused with someone else. That's kind of what I was hoping. At the same time, I *needed* to unravel the mystery.

And then I saw her. *Elsie.* At least she looked similar enough. It had been several years, but I knew her well. I knew that smile well. Those eyes.

My eyes shifted from her picture to her name, back to her picture, repeating the process several times. No way. It was clearly Elsie, but with a different name.

Sydney Porter.

Surely there was some explanation. The different last name was simple enough: possibly a marriage. Maybe she never changed her name back. She had told me that she had never been married, but she might have lied. That would have been a decent reason to be so secretive about her past.

Sure, the different last name could be explained, but why would she have used a different first name? There weren't many reasons. *A boy named Sue* might have changed his first name. No real need to change "Sydney" though.

Maybe I needed to face facts and be honest with myself. The hard truth was that she had lied to me. Time and time again. I needed more information. I needed to know why. I needed to know who Elsie—or Sydney—really was.

I thumbed back to the index for more page numbers featuring *Sydney Porter*. There were plenty. She was popular enough, or at least involved. The two usually went together.

"Oh, Sydney," I said aloud. "What else are you hiding?"

She had been a golfer, a basketball cheerleader, and a tennis player. She had never told me any of this. Actually, I had once caught her swinging my seven iron. Despite her saying that she couldn't golf, I remembered thinking that her swing didn't look half-bad. Actually, she had one hell of a golf swing … I didn't give it much thought at the time—some people are naturals, but her face had reddened. It was as if I'd caught her committing some unforgivable act.

And yes, she was a great athlete, seemingly at everything. In golf, she had placed second at sectionals and advanced to state.

In tennis, she had won her regional, sectional, and she placed third at state.

Unbelievable.

Her smile was the same in every picture. It was the same smile that had greeted me in Leadville. A smile that had quickly been replaced with her initial hesitation after I approached. Maybe she hadn't meant to smile at me. Maybe it was an instinctual response. What if she had intended to remain hidden from the world?

Elsie . . . *Sydney* . . . was clearly hiding something. She was clearly living a secret life.

But what had she done?

I closed the yearbook and pushed it away from me. My default impulse was to grab a drink, but I couldn't do that. Not after what had happened last time. I'd thought about looking outside the window, to see if Ally's lights were on, but I knew that I needed to stay far away from her.

It was time for a drastic change when it came to my coping mechanisms. No impulsive drinking. No impulsive walking into a townhome behind a student.

So instead, I stared into empty space.

Elsie wasn't Elsie. She was Sydney Porter. She had lived in an affluent suburb of northern Chicago—Northbrook. She had *dominated* most of the state in golf and tennis. She was an incredible specimen. Aside from her athletic accolades, she had also been named to honor societies and received numerous academic recognitions. But I'd known none of this.

I needed to discover who my girlfriend really was. I kept turning over my discovery, kicking myself, wondering how I could have known so little about her past.

Well, she was gorgeous. That helped. But she also had an amazing personality. Seriously, why would her past really even matter? Some people get hung up on someone's past so much that it ruins the present.

Plus, in some ways, I knew Elsie better than anyone else. I knew her favorite foods, her mannerisms, her moods, her different smiles, and her precise sense of humor. I wondered if that was better or worse. It was what really mattered to me. I didn't care where she grew up, didn't care where she went to school or if she had been captain of the cheerleading team.

She had been captain for three years.

I didn't know her entire past, but I knew who she was. I convinced myself that that was more important. I convinced myself that I had been doing the right thing by backing off whenever she said that she didn't want to talk about her past. I had respected her privacy and hadn't pried.

A thought hit me: I wondered if Sydney Porter had worked at Arapahoe Memorial. Something told me that they would have no record of Sydney either. If she was running from someone, she wouldn't have given her real name to anyone—if Sydney was even her real name. For all I knew, she had committed a crime spree in junior high and had to change her name then.

I wanted to trust her—to at least see the good in her, but maybe she was one of those people who could earn the trust of anyone. Maybe it was her eyes, her *genuine* warmth. At least it had always appeared genuine. Genuine enough, anyway.

Then again, if I thought hard about her, about the time we had spent together, maybe I'd allowed some of her less-desirable traits to slip through the cracks ... And after several months, I'd definitely noticed some. The longer you know someone, the more you pick up on their production. Their charade. Everyone does the same thing, it's only natural to an extent. Pretending to be the person who they think the other person will dig, or at least tapping into that a little more.

It was all so hard to believe. I looked back through all of her pictures in the yearbook, studying them, pleading for an answer, but all I saw was her smiling face and her name, Sydney Porter.

In the candid shots, she was always surrounded by friends. So yeah, I guess she was very popular.

Her friends.

Hope surged. Elsie Morton might not have any friends, but Sydney Porter sure did. If I could track down one of her friends, I'd surely be able to get some answers. Not only about who Elsie really was, but where she might be.

I'd been ready to doze off, but with a new shot of life, I was ready to work. I began scribbling on my notepad. I noted all of the page numbers where she was pictured with friends. If there were captions, I'd also take down their names. She always seemed to be with two or three different girls.

There was Daria Patel, Julia Tokareva, and Carina Xavier.

She seemed to be closest to Julia. They also looked the most alike. They were both tall with blonde hair, almost inseparable based on the pictures.

Looking at the pictures, I felt like I was looking at a stranger, even though it was my girlfriend. Her smile was different. More genuine? More innocent? She'd let that smile shine through occasionally, but usually only when her guard was completely down. Too often, her smile was a mysterious, restrained grin.

I looked into Julia first. I plugged her name into Google, but I didn't find anything current. She popped up in a few articles from when she was back in high school. I didn't dig too deeply. Then I decided to try Facebook. That's usually the best way to find someone these days.

I typed in her name, pressed enter, and there she was ... Julia Tokareva. I finally had something else to go on. I'd finally learn more about who Elsie really was. I just didn't know whether or not I was ready for that.

Eighteen

Julia Tokareva's profile was highly restricted. I couldn't see her friends or any of the posts on her wall. The only images available were her current profile picture and two past profile pictures. She looked similar in all three of them. They looked like older pictures, but maybe she hadn't aged much.

Before checking her "About" section, I went ahead and sent her a friend request. I debated sending a message, but I decided to wait. I wasn't sure what I'd say yet.

Her "About" section indicated that she was from Chicago, and that she currently lived in New York City.

Shit, I muttered to myself. I couldn't imagine trying to track her down in Manhattan or one of the other Boroughs.

New York City was all I had to go on. No pictures of her in the city or in any particular neighborhood. No mention of where she might have worked. She had kept her profile secret for some reason. If Elsie was running, maybe Julia was, too.

I let out a rush of air and stood. I needed a good stretch. And something to eat. My meals had become few and far between. I was shedding weight.

I was able to find some oatmeal. I popped it in the microwave, then spooned in some chunky peanut butter (only the insane prefer creamy) and blueberries. It actually tasted pretty good. As I stirred my concoction, my phone beeped.

It was a Facebook notification:

Julia Tokareva would like to connect with you.

She hadn't accepted my friend request, but she had sent me a message on Facebook Messenger.

She had gotten in touch very quickly. I'd simply sent her a friend request and she had sent me a message. It made me wonder if Elsie had talked to her about me. It didn't seem natural to message a random guy who had just added her. Maybe she wanted to vet me before accepting the friend request.

I was nervous about checking her message, not sure why. Maybe because I felt myself turning down an ominous road.

I finally clicked on the notification and read her message:

I'm sorry, but do I know you?! Don't take that the wrong way. I'm just very careful about who I add on here!

Her answer was innocent enough. I wondered why she was *very careful* about who she added. It could have simply been a normal safety precaution, but considering Elsie's disappearance, I feared what they might have been caught up in.

My fingers danced above my phone, debating how I was going to answer Julia.

Instead of replying, I dug into my food.

I wasn't sure how much I should say. What if Julia and Elsie had ended their friendship, and what if Julia was the reason why Elsie had changed her name? What if Julia had become obsessed with Elsie and stalked her?

It seemed ridiculous to consider, but it was also unbelievable that Elsie would have completely disappeared from my life. I felt like I needed to be careful about what I disclosed to Julia.

I finally responded:

You might not remember me, but I knew a couple of your friends in high school.

Hopefully, this would be enough to hook her, make her not write me off as some creep.

I didn't have to wait long for a response.

Oh, really?! That's cool! Who did you know?

Before I could respond, she added:

I haven't been in Chicago for years.

I lost touch with most of my friends back there. They probably don't even remember me. Lol.

I was definitely wondering what she was running from, or what kind of mystery I was getting myself into.

Once again, I wasn't sure how to respond. I couldn't throw Elsie's name out there yet. Actually, I'd have to refer to her as

Sydney or else Julia *probably* wouldn't have any idea who I was talking about. Maybe not. Who knows?

I responded: *Carina Xavier. We were both golfers. I met her at a coed event. She might not have said anything about me, but I might have checked out her Facebook several times. Haha… That's where I saw you, and I figured, what the hell?*

I reviewed my message before sending. I would have met Carina more than ten years ago—if I were telling the truth. That would be a long time ago to be trying to track her *or her friends* down. Would that even make logical sense?

Eh. Yeah, people do that. They definitely add old high school crushes to Facebook. They definitely randomly message said crushes after even twenty years of not communicating with each other. Time is so relative.

I sent the message and waited for her response.

Her image popped up next to my message. She had seen it. I waited a little longer, simply eying the message log. No ellipses popped up to indicate that she was typing. A minute or two later, Messenger showed that she was now inactive.

I couldn't sit and wait there forever, so I polished off the rest of my oatmeal and tossed my bowl into the sink. After eating, I hopped in the shower. Once again, marveling at the absence of all of Elsie's things.

After showering, I dried myself off, tossing my towel onto my bathroom floor. I stood naked in my bedroom, glancing toward my phone. As if on cue, it beeped. My screen lit up, glowing in the predominant darkness of my bedroom.

It displayed two short messages from Julia Tokareva:

That's cool!

Did you know Sydney Porter?

Nineteen

I inhaled sharply. Closed my eyes. Let out a long exhale. Julia had basically skipped over the information about Carina and jumped straight to asking about Sydney. Again, I wasn't sure why. I thought back to my concern that Julia might have been a crazy stalker. I'd have to be careful. I definitely couldn't disclose too much information. There were too many ways this could go. I also realized that Julia still hadn't accepted my friend request. So much of her profile remained hidden from my view.

I briefly considered what she might have been keeping me from seeing. If I could see her profile, I'm sure there would be more answers. Maybe.

Or maybe I didn't want to see those answers.

I typed: *A little bit. Are you friends?*

She waited a while to respond. I was starting to get antsy after the ten-minute mark, but then she began typing again. Seconds later, she had responded.

We can't talk on here.

And then she was typing again. Then she stopped for a while. About the time I was about to type a response, Messenger reflected that she was typing. This time it took closer to a minute before she had stopped typing and I had a response.

Look, it's a long story, but there's something that you really need to see in New York. Meet me at Jostle. It's off Columbus, Upper West Side.

I stared at her response, baffled. She wanted me to meet her in New York City? That didn't make any sense, but I also needed to find out about Elsie. I might have been walking into a trap, but what reason would Julia have to trap me?

New York City? When? That's a hike for me…

I debated saying I lived in Denver, but something kept me from sharing that information.

She responded almost immediately.

Like I said, you'll really want to see this. If you know Sydney.

I sighed, looking at the words until they became a blur. It seemed too crazy to go to New York, to meet with an old friend of Elsie's—who knew what kind of relationship they still had?

She might have also been involved with Elsie's disappearance, as crazy as that sounded. Maybe I was losing my mind.

But I couldn't meet with her. There was no way. I didn't know what she planned on showing me, but it was too far.

I can't make it to New York. Sorry.

It showed that she was typing a few times, but I didn't receive a response. Not even after looking at my phone for a few more hours. Not even until I finally fell asleep while still waiting.

Twenty

After waking the next day, I had a notification.

Julia hadn't sent me another message, but she had accepted my friend request. This gave me pause. I wondered just how much information I had on my page ... I think I'd listed that I worked at Washington High School, so she knew that I worked in Centennial. She definitely knew I lived in Denver.

Again, maybe I shouldn't have had her as a friend in the first place. But why would there be any reason to suspect that? I did have thoughts that maybe she was obsessed with Elsie, and that maybe that's why Elsie had had to change her name and run away. But I mean, that was more of just insane thinking. Like, what would be the odds of that actually happening?

So, I had no idea who this was. Maybe it really was Julia, but it seemed so weird that she would tell me to meet her in New York, and then go completely silent when I said that I wouldn't be able to make it.

Then she sent me a message:

Sorry! I got a little busy last night. So, you live in Denver? That sounds amazing. I've always loved the mountains.

Maybe I could meet you there?

Now I was in a panic. She was going to come out here? And now she definitely knew where I lived. Whomever she really was. *She's Julia,* I tried to tell myself, but I was getting paranoid.

I quickly jumped to Julia's Facebook page. I wanted to see what she might have on there.

Anxiously, I scanned. But there was nothing … nothing more than what I'd seen before. A few more pictures were now visible, but there was no personal information. Nothing at all.

Obviously, by design.

For some reason, her page seemed like a trap. She had asked about Sydney. Maybe someone was trying to track her down. They surely didn't have her if Julia asked if I knew her. Or did they just want to see how much I knew about Elsie and what might have happened?

I felt like it was beginning to unravel. At least I had more information to go off of. Not sure if that was ultimately better or worse.

I didn't want Julia to keep looking around my page so I went ahead and blocked her. I'm not sure what difference that really made. At this point, *Julia*—and anyone with her—already knew where I worked.

Then again, I wouldn't be around Washington High School anymore. I had to remember that I'd been suspended. I still couldn't believe that I'd hooked up with Ally …

After snapping out of a daze, I looked at Horace Qualls's Facebook page. We didn't have any mutual Facebook friends. We might have had Elsie as a mutual friend before I'd added Horace, but any trace of Elsie on Facebook had long been erased.

Or maybe … Maybe there were untagged pictures of Elsie on Horace's page. With a little hope, I started looking through Horace's pictures.

I began scrolling. Horace had clearly done well for himself as an accountant. It looked like he enjoyed skiing; he had pictures from Aspen, Vail, Tahoe, Alta, and Telluride.

He also had pictures with his kids. He looked like quite the family man. And on the other end of the spectrum, there were some pictures that looked like some kind of a work, Christmas party. He looked to be pretty liquored up in those.

Horace was just a regular guy living in the city, enjoying the outdoors, enjoying drinks, enjoying his family, and friends. Nothing out of the ordinary.

I was about to give up, but then I saw her. No, it wasn't Elsie. It wasn't Julia.

It was Daria—one of the other friends from the yearbook pictures. It took me a second to register her face; I'd almost mindlessly scrolled past her picture.

She was kind of wedged between Horace and another woman. A smaller man was on the other side. Yeah, I thought for sure it was her. I looked at the tag but it wasn't her name.

Imagine that, I thought, *someone else is lying about her name.*

I realized that I hadn't looked up in a while so I glanced around me to ensure that I wasn't being watched—that nobody was closing in on me. I felt like I had to have some sense of security now that I was in the airport and well past security.

Nonetheless, after being chased through the streets of New York, I was a little on edge.

I checked out Daria's *name:*

Amy Bollinger.

I clicked on her profile. Somehow, I already knew that I wouldn't find anything. Yes, her profile was heavily restricted. I couldn't even add her as a friend. What's more, she didn't even have a picture of herself on her profile.

But I could send her a message. I decided to put it all out there to avoid dragging it out too long and to ensure that she would respond to me. It took me a minute, but I crafted a message for Amy Bollinger:

Hey, this is random, but I've been dating your friend, Sydney Porter, except her name is Elsie Morton now. She must have changed it after high school. I'd talked to someone who claimed they were Julia Tokareva, but I got the impression that it was a fake profile. She tried to get me to go to

New York City to meet with her, and then once she accepted my friend request, she said she would meet with me in Denver.

I'm trying to find out what happened to Elsie. She disappeared one day when I came home from work. Everything was gone. Her Facebook account was deleted. All of her pictures were gone. It's crazy.

I noticed you on Horace Qualls's Facebook page, and I recognized you from your yearbook pictures.

Could you please help me out here? Do you know Elsie? Or Sydney? Do you know where she is? Please. Thank you.

It took a little editing, but I finally pressed enter. I wasn't sure if she was even accepting messages from non-friends, but merely accepting messages couldn't subject her to anything. Unless she didn't trust her curiosity.

I thought back to Elsie, how I didn't know if she was even alive. She could have been dead. She might have been murdered, and someone might have tried to wipe any evidence of her from the world. Or maybe she was being held somewhere.

Amy had already responded:

Julia and Sydney are both dead.

Twenty-One

ELSIE

I'm going to die.

The thought hit me, not for the first time, but I definitely had a feeling that it was going to happen soon.

I'd always feared that getting involved with Mark would be my downfall. It had all been too perfect. Randomly meeting him in a small Colorado town—Leadville, in the valley below where I'd been staying. I hadn't meant to meet anyone, but his alluring charm had disarmed me.

At first, I'd denied his advances. I thought I needed to, but I finally decided to see him again after we had met at the bar.

Mark seemed like one of the good ones. Of course, I also

pushed him away several times. This type of game was new for me, after being on the road for so long. I'd been so afraid of getting too close. But Mark always gave me the space I needed, when I needed it.

And I needed a lot.

I finally gave in and melted into him, allowing myself to give in to my feelings. And it was the biggest mistake of my life. I had made mistakes in my past, but those weren't going to kill me, at least not directly.

Indirectly, it was those mistakes that led to this one.

I needed to focus. I needed to get out of our picture-perfect life in suburbia. The shit wasn't real. It couldn't be.

And if I didn't die first, I was going to end up killing Mark. Hell, I'd murdered a boyfriend before. Not many people have that on their CV …

Looking back, it was Sydney Porter's fault. She needed to die. She needed to be completely erased.

I laughed at the thought.

Fucking Sydney.

I walked down the sidewalk, past our apartment, shielded by the trees above. It wasn't like Mark would see me now, anyway. He was at work. I couldn't help but glance across the street at that girl's house.

Ally.

I remembered the day that she had stopped me on the street, after I'd gotten home from work. Sometime back in October.

"Elsie, wait!" she had yelled.

She jogged up to our front door, smiling. Her cheeks slightly reddened from the early winter chill.

"Hi," I said. "Ally, right?"

I wasn't sure that we had ever said more than a passing hello to each other.

"Yeah, that's what they call me," she said, studying my face.

"Mark's your teacher, right? Mr. Wallace? I think he's mentioned you before."

She went somewhere for a moment. It was difficult to read. It was some combination of anger and disbelief—maybe disappointment, but then her eyes lit up.

"Yeah, I know Mark," she said.

I wondered why she didn't call him, "Mr. Wallace." There was something about the way she had said his name, like she had called him that before. There was definitely a song to it.

"Yeah, I know," I said. "Like I said, he's talked about you."

"What does he say?" she asked, her eyes now twinkling.

I cleared my throat, hoping that would be enough for her to take the hint. "My boyfriend says that you're a great student, that you're very intelligent."

She grinned. "Mark is sweet." And then her expression changed a little, and her tone became more aggressive. "Isn't he the sweetest man you've ever known? I bet you love him more than anyone else."

"What did you want, Ally?" I asked, sharply, trying to ignore what she had just said. *How was I supposed to answer that?*

"Just tell Mark that Ally said hi," she said, and then she smiled at me for an extended second before turning back to her house. Before she cleared the other side of the road, she looked back. "Oh, and tell him that I'll see him tomorrow." She just stood there watching me, and then she started laughing. She shook her head and took off toward her house.

Twenty-Two

MARK

Before I could react to the news that Julia and Sydney were both dead, Amy had sent me another message:

Please don't make me relive this.

And then she sent me a link before blocking me. I knew that I'd been blocked because I no longer had an option to reply.

The link sent me to a random message board where people were talking about a mysterious death that had occurred in a northern suburb of Chicago … Lake Forest. Apparently, it was believed that a young woman had overdosed.

Julia Tokareva.

My heart beat out of my chest upon seeing Julia's name on

the message board. Elsie's best friend had died shortly after high school. That is, if this message board was to be trusted. It could have all been fabricated. But why?

I looked for confirmation, but her death wasn't mentioned anywhere else. I tried Google again, but I didn't find anything.

I went ahead and dove deeper into the message board. They were filled with conspiracy theories. Some were crazy, claiming that the mafia was involved. Someone even thought it was premeditated murder. Someone allegedly close to her.

I froze. Tunnel vision on the computer screen. Everything else was blurred. And warm.

Did this mean anything? Maybe it was somehow connected. Could Elsie have been responsible? There was no way, it had been so long ago. But maybe it was why Elsie had changed her name? I wasn't sure that really made sense, but if a friend had died … And if nobody knew who was responsible …

Julia had been only twenty-one. I tried to find any mention of Sydney, but I couldn't find anything. Nothing.

What about Carina? Was she also dead? The odds were strongly against that, but the odds were also small that my girlfriend had previously had a different last name, and that her best friend had died.

Searching for Julia and Daria had given me some info, but it had also left me with dead-ends. I began digging into Carina. Thankfully, during my initial search, I didn't see any articles about another untimely death. Maybe Carina had also changed her name. I'd need to find her to learn more about Elsie, especially considering Daria thought she was dead.

Once again, I was able to find Carina by searching the mutual friends of other people who were in her class. She had also tried to remain hidden, but the old, reliable, Horace Qualls had come in handy once again.

I discovered that Carina lived in Chicago. If I could find her, she might be able to provide more answers. Julia's death really bothered me. It seemed crazy, but I felt like I didn't have any other options.

I was now periodically sipping from a beer. I really needed to stop drinking. I didn't want to get drunk and do something stupid, but I needed the fuel to keep me going.

Facebook was already open in my browser. I saw that Ally was online. She usually was. I hovered over her name. If I asked, she'd probably come over within a minute.

No. I couldn't.

With some effort, I pushed that thought back. What had gotten into me? How could I have done that to Elsie? How could I continue to have these thoughts about Ally? I really needed to stop drinking. With that thought, I polished off one beer and opened another.

I closed Facebook, focused my mind, and opened Google.

Once again, I reminded myself that Elsie was really Sydney. I searched for Sydney Porter. It was actually a halfway common name. I guess when there are seven billion people in the world, there's bound to be some overlap.

Apparently, there was a writer named William Sydney Porter who used O. Henry as his pseudonym, but he had nothing to do with the Oh! Henry candy bar, *but* the creator of the candy bar was named Williamson.

That wasn't helping me. Most of the "Sydney Porter" results dealt with him. I searched her name along with a few other words such as, "Chicago," "mysterious disappearance," and "murder."

Still, just about every result related to O. Henry. Apparently, he had lived in Chicago and had done three years in prison for embezzlement. When I left Chicago off the search, there was another Sydney Porter who murdered someone in Oregon—this Sydney Porter was an older man, but I was beginning to dislike her name. It didn't have the best associations.

After searching her name and high school, I found some articles relating to her athletic and academic accomplishments, but absolutely nothing else. I even tried her name, "death," and "obituary." Maybe she had faked her death?

Nothing. Actually, including death got me back to O. Henry.

I was suddenly craving the candy bar … Do they even still make those? I didn't think I'd ever actually had one.

I sighed and finished another beer. I went to the fridge for another one. I brought two back. I needed to save trips, conserve energy. I had a feeling that I'd need my strength.

The cans were freezing in my hand, almost making me drop them. I popped the top, took a large drink, then fell back into the couch.

I closed my eyes, wondering where to go from here.
Find Carina Xavier.

Twenty-Three

MARK

My phone woke me. I grabbed it without looking and answered, praying that it was Elsie or someone who knew what had happened to her.

It wasn't, but it was another woman whom I loved.

My sister.

She was going to put my niece and nephew on the line for a video call. I told her to hang tight while I put on some clothes.

"Is everything okay?" my sister had asked.

"What? Yeah, why do you ask?"

"Because it's almost noon, and you were still sleeping," she said, with a little humor in her voice.

She caught on quickly. I'd been in such a great routine in the last several years, ever since I stopped drinking (as much), and ever since I'd moved out to Colorado.

"Yeah, I'm fine," I said, trying to laugh it off. "I'd woken up earlier and took a little nap."

"Kids, come over here," she yelled, off the phone. "Uncle Mark is on the phone."

"Are you ready?" she asked, obviously not too worried about my previous response—or maybe just focused on wrangling up the kids.

"Sure," I said.

Ethan popped onto the screen, followed by Ella. They were both smiling, living lives without any real worries. Not yet.

"See my dino?" Ethan asked, proudly displaying a large stegosaurus.

"Yeah, that's nice," I said, smiling. The kids always made me feel better, no matter how I'd been feeling before.

"Where is Aunt Elsie?" Ella asked. "I wanted to show her my new shirt."

My sister whispered to Ella. "I told you, Aunt Elsie isn't going to be around for a while." Ella's face drooped. And then Melissa turned to me. "I'm sorry, Mark."

"No, it's okay," I said to my sister, and then I said to Ella, "Aunt Elsie will be back soon." It didn't look like Mel or Ella believed me. And about that time, Ethan started ramming the stegosaurs into Ella's head.

"Ethan!" Melissa yelled. "Stop hitting your sister's head!"

"She hit me earlier!" Ethan protested.

"Ugh, give me a minute," my sister said.

I told her that was fine and that she could call me back when she had time. She had clearly seen the Facebook post and probably also believed that Elsie had simply left me. At least, I kind of hoped that's what she believed and not anything worse. I'd always thought my sister had been in my corner before, but who the hell knows?

While I waited for my sister to call back, I knew that I needed to call Carina—I thought I'd found her employer on LinkedIn. But I was delaying the phone call. Maybe I didn't want to know the truth about what had happened before.

Before I could muster up the courage to call, my sister called back. She apologized for the kids, but then she asked, "So, umm, what's going on? I saw your post on Facebook. Why didn't you tell me that Elsie was missing?"

I appreciated that she said "missing" instead of "left you."

"Sorry, I've just been out of it. And I really don't know what's going on," I said. I wasn't sure how much I wanted to say, but I'd already disclosed quite a bit in my Facebook plea.

But at the same time, there were some things I hadn't revealed, such as calling the hospital and being told that they had no record of Elsie ever working there. My sister also didn't know that I'd just been fired. *Or that I'd hooked up with a student. Again.*

"Well? Talk to me."

"Elsie is gone," I said.

Brief pause. "Well, I know that, but like, what happened? Do you have any idea? Any leads?"

"No idea. Like I said on Facebook, everything was just gone. She was gone."

I realized that I was just pacing the floor of my room. I wanted to share how many times I went back and forth already.

"Um," my sister said. "Hey, don't do that!"

"What?" I asked.

"Don't pull your sister's hair! Sorry, they're back at it."

"It's fine," I said. I debated telling her about Elsie's fake identity, but I feared that would make her think I was crazy. She might not believe it, but she might also wonder who I'd gotten involved with and why I didn't know much of anything about her. I didn't want my sister to think less of me because of that.

Melissa said, "Well, hey, I need to go. I was just wondering what the hell was going on. I saw that message and figured I'd check in with you to make sure everything was okay. And I'm sorry, I don't know if I actually asked, but are you okay?

I laughed. "Now, that's a good question. I guess. Even if she left, and if I knew that that's what happened, then I feel better. At least I would know. The hard part is not knowing for sure what happened to her or where she might be. I'm worried about that more than anything."

"I'm sorry, Mark. I love you, and just like the last time crazy shit happened, you know I'll always be here for you."

"Thanks, Mel. I love you, too."

"I guess we'll see what happens. Take care of yourself. Hey, tell your uncle you love him. Tell your uncle bye-bye."

"Bye, Mark!" Ethan said. "Love you!"

"Love you," Ella added.

I told the kids that I loved them and ended the call.

I was still wearing out the carpet in the bedroom. I finally slowed down my pace. I tossed my phone onto the bed. I collapsed alongside with it just looking up at the ceiling fan. Wondering what in the hell I was going to do.

At least I had my sister and my niblings. That phone call had definitely made me feel a little better, but in the end, the call was just another escape.

I needed to call Carina.

It took me another hour, but I finally looked up where Carina supposedly worked and dialed the number. I had flashbacks to calling Arapahoe Memorial (and all of the other Denver-area hospitals) and being told that Elsie Morton didn't work there.

"Winston, Lowell, and Minden. Chicago office. How may I direct your call?"

"Yes, my name is Mark Wallace. May I please speak with Carina Xavier?"

"Let me see if she is available. Are you a client?"

"Prospective," I said. "I hear she's the best."

"Great. One moment, please."

I was placed on hold. I smiled at the music. I instantly recognized the song. It was "Nuvole Bianche" by Ludovico Einaudi. One of Elsie's favorites. She'd said that it always helped her calm down, and it had always made me relax.

The music cut off. My heartbeat sprinted.

"Carina Xavier, how may I help you?"

"Yes, hello, my name is Mark Wallace," I said. I'd rehearsed what I was going to say, but it was a little different with one of

Elsie's old high school friends on the phone. I couldn't believe that I was talking to someone who probably knew more about Elsie's past—all of that info that I knew next-to-nothing about.

"How may I help you, Mr. Wallace?" she asked with a chime to her voice.

"I'm actually calling about an old high school classmate of yours. Her name was Sydney Porter."

There was a long silence. Almost painfully awkward. I was about to continue, but she spoke first.

"Sydney? Who are you again? Why are you calling about her? What do you want?"

I cleared my throat. "I wanted to know more about her past. I'm actually dating her, but her name is Elsie now."

"No, that's not true," Carina said, her voice now coming out sharp, almost angry.

I was taken aback. I wasn't sure how to respond to that. But if Elsie had been running, then who knows what Carina believed about her.

"Sydney is dead. She died more than ten years ago." A brief pause. "Please don't call here again."

And with that, she hung up. I wasn't sure what she believed, but I knew that I needed to get to Chicago. I needed to track Carina down and learn more about what might have happened to Els. Two of her old friends thought that she was dead.

I needed to know why.

Twenty-Four

ELSIE

They would both pay. Soon. Mark and Horace. If only Horace could have left well enough alone. Ultimately, I was to blame. I'd tried so hard to keep even the smallest details hidden. Most had been. And it would have been okay to let a detail slip if there wouldn't have been any reason to reveal them to the world.

I only had myself to blame. Not true. I also blamed Horace for believing that he needed to reach out to Mark. Maybe he felt like he was helping me?

Who knows?

Horace had been a former high school classmate. I'd randomly run into him several months ago while grabbing food in

Denver. I usually never stuck around the same places or became a regular, not wanting to draw attention to myself.

Many times, I'd even give a *different* fake name if I was ordering food somewhere. This time though, I hadn't. I'd given the cashier at Shake Shack my "real" name of Elsie.

And there he was … Horace Qualls. I recognized him instantly. He did a doubletake, raising his eyebrows, knowing it was me but not being able to reconcile the name. I couldn't quite leave fast enough.

He had approached, said that I looked just like someone he went to school with. And then he'd said, "It's you, isn't it? *Sydney Porter*? What do you do, give them a fake name to spice up your life?" And then he laughed, but it was cut short.

He had known everything about my past. He probably feared he had put his own life in danger.

I couldn't even lie to him. He obviously knew it was me. And so, it came to be that someone from my past knew that I lived in Denver. One person. One harmless person that I graduated high school with. Maybe I should have immediately tied up that loose end, but I didn't want to draw attention to myself. I'd tried to believe that it would all work out—that I'd be severely overreacting if I killed Horace. At least back then.

Back in the present, it had all come full circle. Horace's life was in imminent danger, just like Mark's.

Horace was sitting inside the same Starbucks where he had met Mark. I was watching him, but I was also keeping a close watch on my surroundings so nobody would sneak up on me.

The hunter can so quickly become the hunted.

It was mid-afternoon, so the flow in and out of the coffee shop was nearly continuous. Cars hummed by in the drive-through. *Welcome to Starbucks, what can I get started for you?*

Flurries danced on a light breeze; strands of hair blew across my face. I didn't care. I let them stray. I was too focused on Horace. He kept looking around the crowded room. If he was doing anything shady, I wondered why he would do it in such a public place.

After looking around for a few seconds, he would return to his computer, type a few words, then look up again. He was so unfocused and distracted, but I couldn't blame him. He had great reasons to be nervous.

I had what I needed to know. It was time to move before one of two high-profile groups descended on me, trying to capture me for killing people. I also needed to avoid raising any suspicion when the inevitable happened to Horace.

I made it out to my front range cabin that I'd rented off of Airbnb. A light snow danced through the air, collecting against the windows.

The cabin was cozy and would hopefully keep me safe. I tossed another small log on the fire, watching the flames briefly diminish at the moment of impact only to resurrect after eating through the added fuel.

A worn-out couch sat opposite the fireplace. It tempted me to lie down, to take a load off. A nap would be nice, as I had only slept a few hours the night before. Too many thoughts, too much to consider. But I finally concluded that it was now or never. It was time to scheme.

The snowfall had intensified. I couldn't see the same trees I had seen just moments before. A chill overtook me, even though I was standing next to the crackling fire.

The fire reminded me of home. Back in Northbrook. A place I hadn't been for so long. Fire can be comforting, a beacon of warmth and security. But it can also be quite the opposite—a weapon. A destructive, consuming force that can rip through the sturdiest of buildings, claim the most resilient flesh, leaving nothing but charred ruins.

I focused on the dancing flames. If someone could see my eyes, they would see a reflection of hellfire. The eyes are the windows to the soul, right?

We're all a product of circumstance.

I blinked hard, snapping myself out of a daze. I turned back to the window, taking in my faint reflection. A sheen of sweat had formed on my forehead, just below my hairline.

I finally gave up my fight against my fatigue and went into the bedroom. The couch looked welcoming enough, but the bed was actually extremely comfortable.

I instantly fell asleep and was transported back to Chicago. I viewed everything in the eyes of *Sydney* ... A stranger to me.

Sydney Porter ran and ran. Faster than she ever thought possible. She opted to dart through yards as opposed to following the winding roads or sidewalks. Each yard was meticulously cared for, her only concerns were tripping on a sprinkler or tripping a security alarm.

She couldn't draw any attention to herself.

They would never catch her; they could never catch her. What had she done? She would never forgive herself. The gunshots. The screams, the blood. The sight of the bodies.

They were bleeding out. She was directly responsible for five deaths. No, not because of any indirect action. She had pulled the trigger. Multiple times.

If she was ever caught, she would surely be strapped down in a chair, pumped full of lethal poison that would give her a quick, painless death. Or was that painless? She wasn't sure. All in all, that might not have been the worst thing in the world. She thought it then, and she would think the same thing in the years to come.

Her side burned more with each long stride. She was so graceful, still in amazing physical shape. But by now she had run at least two miles—in maybe twelve minutes. That was bordering into overkill territory for most people.

But no, she couldn't slow down, if she slowed down, that might give them just enough of an advantage to catch her.

Where would she go? What would she do? She couldn't live her entire life like this, could she? If so, what kind of life would that be? Looking over her shoulder, living off the grid, constantly worried that her past would catch up with her.

She would need to assume a completely new identity. Somehow, someway.

She thought there were people who dealt in that trade. And she had money. Thankfully.

She had plenty of money ...

At first, she had taken one or two stacks of hundreds, just to see if he would notice. He hadn't. He had money in banks around the world—tens of millions, if not more. Why would he notice ten or twenty thousand missing out of his safe? That would be like ten or twenty dollars to most people. Of course, she'd end up taking much more than that.

She had hidden the cash in a wooded area. She'd scoped the place out, done her due diligence. She'd considered placing it all in a separate bank account, but if she became a suspect, she feared that the account might become frozen or that she wouldn't have access. She'd also feared that he might stumble upon the paper trail.

She had a rough idea of where she was going, but she thought it was still at least three miles away. Could she stay on her feet for five or six miles? With the extra shot of adrenaline, she thought nearly anything was possible.

She continued to rip through suburbia.

If only she were back in Northbrook ... Why had she left home? She could have stayed with her parents, in her cozy child-hood bedroom, but no, she and her friends had to rebel back in high school. She had been so damn tired of the expectations. *Healthy, responsible expectations.* But why hadn't she ever realized that before?

It's amazing how the truth can become so painfully visible

when faced with a life-changing event. Priorities shift when people get knocked off of autopilot, when they wake up from their desensitized, trance-like state.

She glanced over her shoulder, still nothing. No sign of anyone, yet she felt that she couldn't let up. She had to do everything right. She couldn't take any chances. *She ultimately would—and it would cost her.*

But not yet.

Sydney Porter needed to make it back to the money, all of the money that she had stashed away until it was time to execute her plan. It would hopefully be enough to live on for a few years. She already knew that she'd be on the run for a while. It was a lot of money, but sometimes, she wondered if she might have been better off dead.

Back in the present, while Elsie slept, the outside door to the cabin screeched open.

Twenty-Five

MARK

I hadn't expected to be boarding a plane for Chicago, but there I was, trying to track down Elsie's friend, Carina Xavier. She believed that Elsie was dead. Maybe she wouldn't be able to help me, but I hoped she knew more. I needed to find some way to speak with her, to discover more about Elsie.

After landing at O'Hare, I took the train into the city. It was cheap, plus it was direct. I also didn't want to deal with any traffic slowing me down.

From my research (stalking), I discovered that Carina lived downtown in the Loop, not far from the Daley Center on Washington Street.

She lived in a high-rise condo complex with a security guard. I wasn't going to be able to just weasel my way in. I'd have to stake it out. Bump into her on the street.

I really hated what I was doing. It didn't feel right. I didn't want to be that guy who flies across the country to harass a woman, but I didn't think I had a choice. This was the only person I knew who had some connection to Elsie, and not just a connection, but they had apparently been good friends.

Before I could further second-guess my mission, I spotted Carina walking toward me. She was dressed smart, consistent with her condo complex and her job as an attorney.

She was about thirty feet away and closing in. I'd planned my opener, but seeing her so close to me was unnerving.

"Carina," I said. "Carina Xavier."

She stopped dead, slowly casting her eyes over me. Her eyebrows furrowed.

"Look," I said. "I just need to ask you a few questions about your friend, Sydney Porter."

"Fuck. It's *you*, isn't it?"

"Please," I said.

She shook her head, scrutinizing me. I could tell that she was very uncomfortable or hurt. She didn't say anything.

Instead, she turned on her heel, ready to run.

"Sydney. She's my girlfriend. She's been missing."

Carina hesitated.

"Please," I said. "I need your help. Nobody will listen to me. They all think I'm insane."

She slowly turned back, a tear running down her cheek.

She stared at me for a moment, then finally said, "Sydney Porter is dead. She died a long time ago."

"No, she's not. I swear."

"Why are you doing this to me? Is this a sick fucking joke?"

"She's alive. She's lived with me in Colorado, except her name isn't Sydney Porter. It's Elsie Morton. She must have changed her name."

She dropped her eyes and muttered something that I couldn't understand.

"Why do you think she died? What happened?"

"Sergei," she repeated. This time I understood her. "I need to tell you a story ... But it's long." She hesitated and scanned the passersby. "Is there someplace we can meet later? Tonight? I really need to get to a meeting. I'd blow it off if I knew that this was real and that Sydney might still be alive."

"Sure, sure," I said, understanding her doubt. I'd doubted myself enough. It wasn't a stretch to think that Elsie's friend would be in denial.

We made a quick plan to meet at an Irish pub in the River North area. I would stay in the city as long as necessary to find some answers.

I just hated that I had to wait.

She was keeping something from me, at least temporarily. I just wanted to read her mind and take all of the answers back to

Denver, but I couldn't. I hadn't learned much of anything yet. I had no idea who Sergei was. I was tempted to check the yearbook, but somehow, I already knew that he wouldn't be in there.

Twenty-Six

ELSIE

I woke up to floorboards creaking, finding myself in a deep panic. *Deep breaths, Els. Deep breaths. Calm down. It's okay, it's okay.* But trying to convince myself that there wasn't a threat may have been worse than embracing it. I could then take action and face my problem head-on. The Titanic had already hit the iceberg, it was filling up with water. Foolhardy claims that it was unsinkable—that I was unsinkable—were delusional.

I knew that they had been following me. I didn't think they would be able to track me so deeply into the mountains. It might have depended on how much they knew and how much they had uncovered. Or maybe I simply hadn't been careful enough.

Another floorboard creaked, its cry intensified by the stark silence both inside and out. The falling snow continued to provide a blanket, smothering any noise that would rise from within the cabin.

My phone flashed. Thankfully, I'd silenced it. Not a message though, just a notification that my battery was down to fifteen percent. No signal other than an occasional bar.

The footsteps were now unmistakable, hammering out a path from the table to the kitchen cabinets, then back to the table. A chair was pulled out. It scraped loudly against the wooden floor—letting out a high-pitched screech, but then nothing.

Silence, but the intruder's presence was unmistakable.

I struggled to get my blood pumping again. Shifting my weight could give me away, but I needed to be ready to defend myself. *Or strike first?* It sounded like there was only one person, maybe I would be able to take him or her down. I'd done it before. I'd taken out people who should have outmatched me.

My phone rang. Loudly. My heart rate intensified. I thought for sure that I had silenced it.

Shit. I was done.

No, it wasn't my phone. After a few seconds, I realized the ringtone came from the other room.

Before it was answered, I rolled to the edge of the bed, keeping my feet hovering just above the ground.

A deep voice resonated throughout the cabin, definitely a man. Probably a large man.

"Hallo!" ... "No, no, it's empty." ... "Yah, that's right. It's empty!" ... "Stack of papers on the table. Scribbles on 'em. She must have took off before the storm. You know her." ... "Yeah, yeah, I know. If she shows up, I'll take care of her. Don't worry about none of that."

My feet had come into contact with the cold cabin floor. There was no escaping through the front door, but maybe I could get to a window. It wouldn't be easy; I feared the old floorboards of the cabin would give me away instantly.

The man had said the cabin was empty—for whatever reason. To my knowledge, he hadn't checked the bedroom, the room most likely to be occupied in the middle of the night.

And wouldn't he have seen my car?

Each time the man spoke, I tried to take a couple of steps toward the window. It was the only chance I had. Thankfully, the floorboards had cooperated enough. They made a little noise, but the noise was masked by the volume of his voice.

"Not tomorrow!"

Now only a few feet away from the window ...

"No, she wouldn't be so stupid. And the roads are impossible" ... "Yeah, that's what I said, *impassable*. I barely made it up here in my snowmobile. This is one hell of a storm."

Closer.

The snow had accumulated several inches on the sill. And it was still falling.

"Then be on standby." ... "Yeah, I don't give a shit. I'll pay whatever as long as we take care of her."

My hands pressed against the window pane. Ice-cold, paint

chipping away beneath my fingers. I found a latching mechanism, unlocking the window. Even though it was unlocked, I worried how loudly it would scrape while opening. A window in an isolated cabin might have been closed for months. At least. It was old. It would probably squeal.

I pushed slightly—it gave, quietly. A blast of cold air and snow shot through the room. I tried to coordinate my next movement with the man's next answer.

"As long as you bury her."

My hand slipped when the window was nearly halfway up. Still not enough room for me to climb through.

"What was that? … Heard something. Gotta go."

It was all or nothing. I shoved the window the rest of the way. It let out a loud screech.

A chair tumbled to the floor in the other room, footfalls pounded against the hardwood floor, heading straight for the bedroom.

"Who's in there?" The voice boomed.

In my rush to get the window open, I'd realized that I was ill-equipped to face the wintry elements. Even if I managed to get outside—away from the cabin, I had nowhere to go.

My car was blanketed with nearly a foot of snow. The man had said that the roads were impassable, which I believed. There was no reason not to.

Shit!

Maybe I shouldn't have put myself in a dead-end situation, but I honestly didn't think there was any way they would have followed me out here. It was one of many dead-end options that I had. At least this one, I thought, provided a sanctuary.

The doorknob jangled.

At least I'd locked the door. That would buy me a little time. But not much, judging by the heaviness of the footfalls. The man would probably be able to blast through the door.

"Open up!" A fist thundered into the door.

I hoisted myself up and through the window, falling into the snow on the other side.

Before I could get up, a hand clasped around my shoulder and spun me around. My time had run out.

They'd finally caught me.

Twenty-Seven

MARK

Hours after meeting Carina on the street, I was waiting in the bar, not turning my back to anyone. I wanted to be able to see any threat. Part of me wondered if this was a setup, but I felt like I could trust Carina. I'd seen it in her eyes. She seemed to genuinely believe that her friend was dead.

Both she and Daria had believed it.

I'd tried to spend the afternoon taking in the sights, but it all looked cold and dreary. Maybe that's because it was winter in Chicago. It doesn't quite have the same effect as summer. It's always cloudy and everyone is draped in black coats, struggling to walk against the wind tunnels between the skyscrapers.

It's not quite like winter in Denver. Winter in Denver is actually comparatively mild. Lots of sunshine. And not *too* much snow unless you head out to the mountains. Speaking of which, the storm should have now been hitting the mountains.

I glanced at the weather on my phone. *Yup.*

I also noticed the time. It was already close to 9. Carina was almost an hour late. I had a sickening feeling. What if someone had watched us earlier? What if I was not supposed to speak to Carina? Maybe someone had taken steps to ensure that this meeting would never happen.

Just when I was about to get up and leave, the door opened and Carina walked inside. She scanned the bar, looking right past me before finally locating me on her second pass.

"I need to make this quick," she said, taking a seat across from me. "I've been thinking about Sydney all day. If this is real … It'd be awesome that she's still alive, but you need to understand that she would be in major danger." Her eyes nervously scanned the bar, occasionally landing on me.

She added, "You probably are, too."

"Danger?"

"Sergei was in the Russian bratva."

"What? The Russian bratva?"

"It's basically the Russian mafia. The bratva has major influence in that town. They were able to make it all disappear … But Sergei killed Julia. He gave her the drugs. She overdosed. He didn't do anything to help her. She just laid there and died. He was responsible. We all knew it. Nothing happened, but Sydney played it cool. She tried to comfort Sergei, to be there for him. They dated for a while. I didn't understand at first."

It stung a little to know that Elsie had been dating a member of the Russian bratva. I didn't say anything.

Carina continued. "Sydney started dating him because she wanted to pay him back. She finally let me in on her scheme. He died, and then she was gone. She just completely disappeared. I never heard from her again … I just assumed they found her, killed her, and dumped her body in Lake Michigan."

"Wow," I said, clearing my throat. Stunned. Having only a scant idea of what Elsie may have done between getting close to Sergei and when I met her. "But she's not dead. I swear that she's alive. At least, she was alive just a few days ago. Elsie is the same girl in the yearbook. *Sydney*," I said.

"God, I really hope so," Carina said, shaking her head. "I've thought about her so much, especially after having my kids. I wish she could have met them. She loved Julia's daughter so much … Nataliya."

"She's been great with my niece and nephew, too."

"But you two don't have any?"

"Nope," I said, glancing away, lingering on a young couple at another table. I finally looked back. "So, you never heard from Elsie after Sergei died? Not once?"

She inhaled sharply, her eyes drifting around the bar, perhaps searching for a past memory they had shared, trying to cling to something. I imagined them all hanging out in a bar together after they'd all turned twenty-one, before Julia had died.

Carina's eyes finally landed on me. "Not once."

"Elsie is alive," I said. "And we will bring her back. From wherever she is."

"I hope so, but I'm not going to get my hopes up."

I stared ahead, thinking the same thing.

Carina continued. "You come here and say that my best friend in high school is alive, but she's missing. To me, she's been dead for more than a decade. Yes, I want to believe you. I desperately want Elsie to be Sydney, but I have my doubts. Strong doubts. I'm not sure I could handle having my earth shattered again. Do you know what it's like to lose your best friend at such a young age? It's crushing."

"I can't imagine," I said. "And I'm sorry that you had to go through all of that."

I switched gears, trying to make her believe me.

"When Elsie laughs really hard, she snorts. I think it's because she's trying to hold it in, embarrassed by her laugh. And then she laughs even harder, just letting it all out, until she starts crying. And when she looks at you, you know that she cares. She blocks everything else out. It's just you and her. She stares into your soul. Her eyes are so mesmerizing."

I'd been in a daze, looking toward the bar while recounting some of my memories, ambivalent to Carina. When I turned back to her, she was now smiling, but barely.

She said, "And she was very competitive. I played doubles with her in tennis. She yelled at me whenever I missed a ball. She wanted to win so bad. She was so athletic and smart."

"She loves to snowboard," I said.

Carina grinned. "She did! Our families took trips to Aspen and Vail."

"She does," I said. "Present tense. She loves to snowboard."

"I'm sorry, but I still can't believe it." Carina choked up. "I want to. I trust you, but it's just too much." She couldn't say anything else.

I quickly went to the bar to get some paper towels, keeping an eye out for trouble. The paper towels weren't quite Kleenexes, but they would have to do.

Carina took them and tried to wipe the tears away.

"Her favorite color is baby blue," I said. Carina nodded and sniffled. "It *is*," she said. "It is."

I smiled back at her, but I still felt lost and terrified. Elsie was still missing, and I had no idea where she was.

"We need to find her," Carina said. "I'll do anything to see Sydney again. Actually, I like that name, *Elsie*. It sounds like a fresh, new start. I'll call her that so we're on the same page."

I wasn't sure how much I wanted to drag Carina into everything. Her life would also be at risk. It probably already was. I didn't think I'd be able to keep her away from Colorado.

We parted ways, and I took an Uber from the bar to my hotel. It would have been a relatively short walk, but it was late, the crowds had thinned, and I was slightly paranoid.

From the back seat of the Uber, I tried to make a phone call. Her number was still saved. No image. It had somehow been deleted, but there she was. All that I had left of her.

"Els" and her number.

I smiled. A weak smile. I remembered the first day that I'd put her name and number in my phone, just before we had said goodbye at that Leadville dive bar.

She had been hesitant, but now I understand why. I was beginning to understand much more about her.

I pressed "Call" just to see if by some chance, she was connected to the world. If only I could hear her voice again.

Ding, Ding, Ding, We're sorry, but—

I ended the call.

I tried again.

Same response.

Trying again wasn't going to make any difference. There was only so much that I could actively do. I put the phone back in my pocket and leaned back in my seat, closing my eyes.

I prayed that I'd be able to find her, but I was losing hope. She was out there, somewhere in the world. The only question was if she was dead or alive.

Twenty-Eight

ELSIE

The hand on my shoulder was strong, forceful. I was freezing cold, already weakened by the conditions. I felt like the force would shatter my body into thousands of pieces like a hammer to a block of ice.

"Why did you run away from me?" he asked. "We need to get you back inside the cabin. Then figure out what to do with ya. You silly, silly girl."

Windblown snow whipped through the forest. The trees should have acted as a barrier, but the wind always seems to find a way to tunnel. And when it tunnels, the effect is magnified.

My teeth were chattering, face had to be beet-red. The man

was wearing a black balaclava and a camouflaged snowsuit. He easily went six feet, but that's all I could see.

Was he out here alone? He was the only person I'd heard in the cabin, but that didn't mean much. The others could have been waiting for the right moment to spring into action. But he already had me. It wasn't adding up.

"Come on. I'm not going to hurt you," he said. "I don't want you to freeze out here. *I* don't want to freeze out here." He laughed.

I mentally switched gears and followed him back to the cabin. I was still on guard, as any woman would be when following an unknown man into an isolated cabin.

He quickly had a fire blazing. My papers were still stacked haphazardly on the edge of the table, seemingly untouched.

Maybe he thought I was someone else.

"Warming up?" he asked, removing the balaclava. His face was weathered, might have been in his upper forties. Not what I'd expected.

"Yeah," I said, instinctively drawing toward the fire and away from him.

"I must have scared ya. Didn't think anyone would be up here, cept maybe my wife."

"Your wife?"

"Well, soon to be ex. I was just talking to my lawyer on the phone. He warned me not to come out here, was afraid of what I might do to her. Hell, I guess. I wouldn't have done anything."

"Is this your cabin? I rented it out."

I paid cash. Not traceable. She doesn't have my name.

"Yeah, you probably did. She keeps track of all of that. Always has. Never trusted me with it. I'm just an old, dumb redneck." He laughed. I smiled.

"So, what are you doing out here all alone during this snowstorm?" he asked.

I pulled the blanket a little tighter. "Just wanted to get snowed in. *Thought* it would be peaceful." I raised an eyebrow.

He laughed a little. "I guess I had to ruin your plans. Probably scared you half to death. I just wanted to make sure you didn't freeze. I'm sorry."

"No," I shook my head, "Don't worry about it. You probably saved my life. I'd still be running circles out there. I was afraid you were going to kill me."

The energy may have shifted a little. Either he thought I was afraid of him or he realized that I had someone who actually wanted me dead. All things being equal, there was no reason for him to jump to that conclusion, but all things weren't equal. All things were never equal in my world.

But he clearly hadn't thumbed through my notes. If he had, he would have been more afraid of me.

He smiled weakly. "No, I wouldn't kill anyone. But I am looking forward to burying my wife in our divorce. Guess if you overheard that, it might have sounded bad."

I extended my toes, excited that I had feeling back.

"Do you write?" he asked, motioning toward the table.

"Only when I feel inspired," I said.

He took a step toward the table, my muscles tensed.

I continued, needing to deter him. "Most of it's too personal to ever share with the world."

He stopped. "Well, then I wouldn't want to impose. I'm sure it's great though."

I smiled.

"I'm sure that you're ready for me to get out of your hair. After scaring you to death. Guess I'll be moving along. Hopefully I can make it back down the mountain."

"Good luck."

Twenty-Nine

MARK

Some of it was starting to come together. At least I knew, defin-
itively, that Elsie Morton existed. The trouble was, so did Sydney
Porter. And Sydney Porter had caused a little bit of trouble. At
least I now knew that she wasn't responsible for Julia's death. I
really didn't want to believe that she could have killed her friend,
but some of the surrounding circumstances hadn't looked good.
And then she may have been trying to exact vengeance after her
friend died, but she had messed with the wrong people. Could
she have really killed Sergei?

I'd started digging into Sergei Kalishav's death, as well as the
organization that he was part of. The Russian mafia, also known

as the bratva. His family wasn't a huge player, at least not on the global scene, but they had some clout around Chicago. Many had assumed leadership positions in finance companies, which had recently transitioned to bio and nanotech. Wherever they could use their positions to exert influence.

It was alarming that these kinds of people could so quickly ascend leadership roles in companies. I'm sure they did the same thing in government. Infiltration and takeover from the inside. Always the quickest method.

So, although I had put a few pieces together, the puzzle was still far from complete. What had happened to Sydney Porter after Sergei's death? Had she actually killed him? If so, how? Would she kill again if a guy pissed her off, or was that simply a revenge killing?

I didn't know how much deeper I wanted to dig. I wasn't about to stake out members of the bratva in the hopes of getting answers from them. I imagined that asking them about Elsie could quickly result in my death and/or Elsie's. I briefly considered unblocking *Julia*, but I was now almost completely positive that was a trap.

All of these thoughts came and passed while I was lying on the hotel bed. I'd long since turned the TV off. I was soothed by the hum of the heater, desperately fighting to keep pace with a chilly December night in Chicago. It was doing okay though. All things considered, I also felt okay. I was almost comforted, believing that I was moving closer to unraveling the mystery of Elsie's disappearance.

Just before I nodded off to sleep, there was a light knock at the door. Three light raps, barely enough to register.

My eyes shot wide.

Nobody knew I was in Chicago, other than Carina. Horace might have thought I might come to check it out. I hadn't told my sister or anyone else.

I raised my head slightly, trying to hear anything else.

Nothing.

No more knocking, no scuffling of feet. It was possible that the knocker was still standing there, with a gun aimed at the door. *It was possible.*

Another knock.

This time, I thought I heard a light shuffling of feet, carrying the knocker away from the door, down the hallway. This wasn't a motel; the knocker couldn't have just come in off the street. He or she had to be a guest to gain entry.

"And you want to be my Latex salesman?"

Someone had just turned on the TV in the next room. Just in time for one of Seinfeld's most memorable moments.

Latex ... Latex gloves?

It made me consider a murder-for-hire. Maybe someone had been sent to murder me in my sleep. Maybe I'd gotten too close to discovering a buried secret. *No way.*

Nobody had any reason to murder me . . . unless they were trying to get to Elsie. If she had killed Sergei, then she had definitely messed with the wrong people, and they would surely want vengeance, no matter how much time had passed.

Not comforting. Not at all.

I would have preferred to fall asleep without peeking outside the door, but the temptation was too strong. Plus, my heart was beating too fast. There's no way I'd be able to get any sleep. Not until I scoped this out. I needed answers of some kind, even if it was a bullet to the head.

I threw my legs over the edge of the bed.

No gun. No baseball bat.

My fists were my only weapon.

I looked through the peephole, but I didn't see anyone, nothing but a straight shot to the room across from mine.

Room 432.

As I opened the door, I realized that I should have called the front desk, or the cops. They could have come up here to check it out. But that might have been a little embarrassing once they uncovered that I was imagining things. Because I knew that I probably was. This had to be nothing.

I whipped the door open and cocked my fist back, preparing for anything.

Nobody was on the other side.

I let out a rush of air, then looked each way. I was toward the end of the hall, far removed from the elevator in the middle, farther away from the stairs on the other end. I wouldn't have necessarily heard the person go down the steps.

But I might have heard him enter the room next to me.

I was about to slide back into my room before looking down. And there it was. Just a white sheet of paper, your typical copy paper. There were two lines written in black marker. The second line nearly stopped my heart from beating.

IT IS A BAD NIGHT TO BE IN CHICAGO
HAVE YOU CALLED YOUR SISTER LATELY?

Thirty

ELSIE

Finally, Charles left, and I was alone. My phone, which I'd placed on the charger, showed that it was a little past four in the morning. I couldn't have slept more than an hour or two before Charles showed up at the cabin.

Now, I was up. I would probably crash later in the morning or afternoon, but the shot of adrenaline had kept me from falling back asleep.

Instead, I was still cuddled up on the couch, basking in the warmth of the raging fire. Charles made one hell of a fire; I'll give him that much credit. Otherwise, he's not high on the list of my favorite people.

I couldn't blame him for assuming nobody would be here, not in the middle of such a nasty storm. Nonetheless, to show up in the middle of the night? That's bold.

A more ruthless occupier might have blown his head off. Especially if said occupier was cautiously waiting for her pursuers to catch up with her.

I pulled the cable-knit throw blanket up to my eyes, peering out just over the top. My core temperature was back to normal, but I sought security from the blanket. It was a relatively small barrier from the world, but it would have to do for now.

My eyes skipped from the fire to the window. Snowflakes continued to fall, but they had eased their frantic pace. I continued on, sweeping the room with my eyes, making sure everything was still in order.

I landed on the stack of papers. Blue-lined notebook paper, smothered with black pen.

Hadn't the stack been taller?

My heart skipped a beat. I pushed into the couch with my hands, propping myself up, my upper body turned back toward the table. The right side of my face warmed by the fire, the left side cooled by the haunting realization.

For an extended second, I was frozen—staring at the diminished stack of papers. Wondering if Charles had snooped.

Finally, I gathered my legs and marched across the room. Even if he had taken a few sheets of paper, it's not like he could prove anything. It could have been brainstorming for a book or a screenplay.

Maybe. How detailed had I been?

… Detailed.

The fire was no match to the warmth spreading the length of my body, pressing against my skin. Fear, sure. But also, embarrassment. How could I have been so stupid. Even if I had no reason to believe anyone would come into the cabin, how could I leave that kind of information out in the open?

I reached the table and flipped through the sheets. Yeah, there were definitely some pages missing. *Fuck.* Straight from the top. At least two or three pages. I didn't have them numbered, but I'd numbered the list. The now top page on the stack began with number fifteen.

The information contained within the preceding steps wouldn't have buried me, but in the margins, I wrote so much more. I don't know how many times I had written "KILL HIM."

And Charles was just talking to an attorney. He would probably ask him what he should do with the papers. *Shit.* But I could always write it off, say that I was producing a screenplay—that it was all my creative brilliance. A work of fiction. Actually, that would probably work.

Fuck yeah! No worries!

I collapsed onto the chair, a mixture of crazy-exhausted, relieved, and still kind of scared shitless. I mindlessly sifted through the pages of my scheme.

I shook my head, laughed.

Maybe I would be able to sleep now. Get a few hours in before the sun came up. I knew its rays would come unimpeded through the bedroom window. Any amount would help though. I needed to be on alert.

My knees cracked as I rose from the chair. *Too young for that shit.* Too much mileage on my young frame. I shuffled around the table, turning toward the bedroom. That's when I noticed something out of the corner of my eye, near the cabinet next to the fridge.

Yellow sheets of paper. Three sheets.

That explained the smaller stack.

And then I laughed, opened the door, and dove onto the bed. I was out instantly.

Wading in and out of coherence, my eyes finally closed. Consciously, I wanted to believe that I was safe here. But deep down, I knew that I could never escape my tail. Either way, I was fucking exhausted, so sleep mercifully came.

I wondered if I'd go back to that night in Chicago. I've had those dreams so many times—of that night.

Sometimes, I'd wake up screaming. Mark would ask what was wrong, what I'd been dreaming about, but I could have never shared the details. He would have never looked at me the same, and I wouldn't have blamed him.

Once again, I replayed some of that night in my mind.

Thirty-One

MARK

I stared at the words until they became a blur. It was already well past eleven. I didn't want to wake my sister, but considering the threat in my hands, I needed to make sure that she was okay.

I called her. She answered on the fifth ring.

"Hey, what's up?" she whispered. "It's late."

Now, I couldn't really repeat the threat, that would only scare the crap out of her. I should have thought this through before calling her, but it had been a reflexive reaction.

"Sorry," I said. "I'm in Chicago."

"Chicago? Really? Are you coming down?"

"I can't this time," I said. I wanted to tell her that I flew in for business, but a high school history teacher generally doesn't fly to Chicago for business. "I was meeting a friend."

I didn't say anything else. The line went quiet.

Finally, she said, "Is everything okay?"

"As long as you and the kids are okay. With Elsie gone, it's been hard lately. It takes me back, you know? I start to worry about other people close to me."

"Yeah. I'm sorry. We're all okay. We were looking at old pictures today. They wanted to talk to Aunt Elsie again. I tried to explain it to them again. Maybe I could just say that she's been really busy with work."

Work. I still had no idea if she even worked or what the Arapahoe Memorial charade was about. If the Russians were after her, then maybe she'd simply been laying low. She probably made that up just to feign normalcy.

But where did all of her money come from?

"Brother? Are you still there?"

"Yeah, sorry," I said. "I'm working on finding her. Look," I started. I needed to be honest. I owed it to my sister. "Elsie may have had something happen when she was younger. Some people might have found her."

"What? Who?"

"It's crazy. I'm slowly putting the pieces together."

"Do you think they have her?"

"I don't know. Just promise me that you'll be careful, okay?"

"Mark, please be honest with me," she said, flatly. "I need to know what you know. I need to protect my kids."

I took a deep breath. "I'm at a hotel up here. I was about to fall asleep, but I heard someone knock at the door. I checked it out. They had left a note. It said that it was a bad night to be in Chicago, and it said, *Have you called your sister lately?*"

"Oh, my God," she said, barely above a whisper. "You weren't going to tell me this? What are we supposed to do?"

"I didn't want to scare you," I said, defensively but with a tremor in my voice. I hadn't even given myself much time to process their cryptic threat. "You can call the cops and explain what happened. Maybe they'll watch your house. I'll call them, too, and try to explain everything."

"My God," she said, then repeated it. It sounded like she was up and moving around. "The kids are sleeping. I'm afraid to leave them in their rooms."

I thought of my niece and nephew, lying there, vulnerable. The threat had only mentioned my sister, but I knew that the kids were also in danger. Even if they survived, if something happened to my sister—their mom, they would be forever scarred.

"What do I do?" She sobbed. "I don't know what to do."

"You're going to be okay. I'll call the Edwardsville police right now and explain what happened. I'll tell them it's an emergency. You should also call 9-1-1. Explain that you've been threatened by the Kalishav bratva out of Chicago."

"Kalishav bratva?" she repeated. "What?!"

I hadn't shared that part. Maybe I shouldn't have.

"I think those are the people who left the message. Look, I'd rent a car and drive down there or ask you and the kids to come stay with me, but I think that would be more dangerous."

"Yeah," she said, thinking. "And I can't take them to Mom and Dad's because I'd be risking their lives, too … Shit!"

"I'm sorry," I said.

"It's not your fault," she said, but I'm not sure that's what she believed.

It was my fault. My sister, and her kids, were in danger because of my girlfriend. Because of her past. By any definition, it was my fault, at least to some degree. If I hadn't ever met Elsie, my sister would be sleeping soundly.

I would have also been sleeping soundly.

Granted, I wasn't the root cause, neither was Elsie. If Julia hadn't gotten involved with Sergei, everything would have been different for so many people. It's amazing how one seemingly insignificant event can have such a wide-ranging impact on so many, like the spread of a pandemic from subject zero to millions or billions.

I doubted that this situation would affect so many, but the few lives it had affected carried exponential weight since they were all so close to me—including my own life.

I told her I loved her and she reciprocated. After ending the call, I immediately dialed the Edwardsville Police Department.

I tried to explain everything that had happened and how my sister was in danger. It reminded me of speaking with Detective Brighton and Officer Shaw. I admittedly had next-to-zero proof of anything. I had the note, but they couldn't see it. There was no way to get it down to them. Even then, they might not believe the source. I was sure they wouldn't.

"We can run a cruiser by her place and look into it," the chief had said. At least they had connected me to him. The dispatcher had been concerned enough. "But unfortunately, we really don't have much to go on here."

I thanked them. I also feared that they would eventually connect the dots and realize that I was the same Mark Wallace who had been arrested for killing his girlfriend.

I'd been ignorant of my surroundings during the last two phone calls, simply assuming that the knocker had left after delivering the note.

I glanced at the digital clock, *11:43*.

How am I supposed to sleep after that?

I couldn't. I packed up my things and left, scanning the hall several times before leaving my room. I took an Uber out to the airport and found a late redeye from O'Hare back to Denver.

If anything, I could sleep on the plane. I'd at least be safe and sleep securely at 30,000 feet. Unfortunately, I didn't know if my sister would be so lucky.

Thirty-Two

ELSIE

It was time to leave the cabin. I stepped outside into the frigid morning, in the wake of the snowstorm. Thankfully, the driveway had been plowed. Perhaps Charles had been responsible for that. I trudged through the snow, better dressed for it than I'd been last night. It's not that it really mattered though. I barely even felt the cold.

It would have been best to stay at the cabin for a few more nights. I really didn't want to constantly be moving around, but since Charles had found me, I wondered who else might. I was also too paranoid. What if he had been sent by someone? What if he was going to turn me in because of my notes?

I pulled away from my temporary safehouse. At some point, I needed to stop running and face my problem. Isn't that what they always say? Somehow, I felt that there were varying degrees. Sitting down to do your taxes was a little different than donning armor to battle the Russian bratva.

Either way, I didn't want any more blood on my hands. I wondered what they might do to flush me out. I just hoped they weren't close enough to do any serious damage to anyone. And I missed Mark so much.

Missing Mark was hard enough, but I also thought about his family—especially his sister and the kids. I hoped that they were okay. I didn't know exactly how close the bratva was or what they might try to do.

It was hard not having any kids. I'd wanted a daughter all my life, a mini me, but due to being on the run and considering everything that had happened, I just couldn't do it. If I had a child, he or she would be in constant danger. It wouldn't have been fair. And that's why I'd told Mark that I wasn't ready. Mark seemed so hurt when I'd told him, but he tried to play it off by explaining that he was fine with his niece and nephew.

I wanted to believe that we might be able to have kids someday, but I was already getting to that point where it became much more difficult and riskier.

Like Mark, at least I had Ethan and Ella. I wasn't "Mom," but at least I was "Aunt Elsie." I'd also briefly been an honorary "Aunt" to Julia's daughter all those years ago.

Thinking of Julia was hard. We had been so close. When she

died, I lost a huge part of myself. Everything had already been blurry. I wasn't living the most upstanding life at the time. It all spun. The decision came quickly. I pretended like I didn't blame Sergei—that it was an accident. We healed together. I got in close and when the time was right, I paid him back for taking Julia away from me.

Thirty-Three

MARK

Sydney Porter. Yeah, it's a recurring thought. The name keeps flashing through my head. I see it everywhere. There was a report on ESPN about the retired Pittsburgh Steelers linebacker, Joey Porter, and then I went to McDonald's to grab a sandwich; the cashier's name was Sydney. It was even spelled the same way, not even Sidney. What were the odds of that? Probably not astronomical, but still. Focus is so powerful in this world.

Sydney Porter.

Elsie Morton.

I was about to turn off the TV, but the local news came on. A blonde man with an impressive jawline had just hit his somber button. It was impressive how quickly he could go from a beaming smile to looking like he was at a funeral.

Clearly, their expressions were genuine. Acting. Putting on a different face, just as Elsie had done.

"We have received confirmation of a homicide on the 900th block of Lewiston Street near downtown."

The video cut to the scene. I had a bad feeling even before they plastered the face on the top corner of the screen. I clutched a tuft of my hair, took a deep breath. My stomach was on fire. I wondered if someone knew that Horace had talked. Maybe someone was disappointed in Horace.

Maybe I wasn't supposed to know about Sydney Porter.

And there it was. His name on the screen: *Horace Qualls.*

I collapsed lower into the couch. My head fell down between my hands. I looked back up at the TV, just to make sure I wasn't imagining things. There was no way. I pinched myself, but I continued to see the man's face.

They repeated his name.

Horace Qualls.

It was real, all too real.

Horace was in his lower forties. He had a wife, two kids. Accountant. Skier. He was known to be an upstanding man in the community. Coached his son's baseball team.

Pretty boy Jake continued to drone on about everything else happening in Denver. I shut him off. I stared at the blank screen for several minutes.

How could *my Elsie* have been involved in this?

I shook my head—a developing habit. No, not Elsie. *Sydney.*

I feared that I might be next. I tried not to consider that she was responsible for Horace's death. I didn't want to believe that she changed her name after committing some horrible crime. She was athletic, strong. She had some size. Then again, it didn't take size to kill. The element of surprise, poison. Hell, a gun. There are numerous ways to kill without overpowering them.

I would know. My hands aren't clean.

Elsie was smart enough. I knew that. If I didn't have any verification after being with her, I'd found out by scouring her yearbook. She was brilliant—brilliant, athletic, breathtakingly gorgeous. She was the full package.

She was also a liar. Possibly a manipulator.

But was she a murderer? There's quite a jump between lying and taking another life. Her lies hadn't even hurt me, not in the moment, anyway. She'd lied about her name, but for all I knew, it was a simple white lie. People change their names for many reasons. I really needed to calm down and not let my imagination get away from me. I knew Elsie, didn't I? We had spent so much time together. She couldn't have been a killer.

Then again, she would likely fit several profiles for killers, and intelligence usually puts people over the top. And not just raw intelligence, but real-world smarts.

I couldn't go down that road. It couldn't have been Elsie. She couldn't have kept so much from me. She was simply caught up in something bad. A victim.

Or, maybe Horace's death was completely unconnected to

what he had told me. Maybe what happened in Chicago was also completely unconnected.

What would the statistical probability be?

I sighed and got off the couch. My knee and ankle both popped. That's uncommon for me. The stress was taking its toll. I'd never felt so much stress in my entire life. I wasn't sure how I was supposed to deal with it.

I crossed our living/dining room, into the kitchen. Elsie had always loved to cook late-night omelets. That's another thing she was great at—cooking. Omelets loaded with bacon, onions, green peppers, and mushrooms. She'd also throw in some chili garlic sauce. Damn, they were good.

Opening the fridge, I realized that I hadn't been to the grocery store since losing Elsie. I'd relied on a steady stream of fast food. Yet there was a box of eggs. A few days past the due date, but my mom had always told me that the date really didn't matter for eggs: As *long as they don't look nasty when you crack them.*

Thanks, Mom, I thought.

They looked okay. I cracked four eggs over a bowl. Then I cracked one more, then another. The first five breaks had been clean, but this one shattered in the bowl.

I wiped a tear from my cheek. I missed Elsie.

I didn't care what her name was. I missed her. My girlfriend. *Elsie ... Sydney.* She could have been named anything: *Abigail, Kiersten, Connie.* It didn't matter to me. I didn't love her name; I loved her smile. I didn't love her name; I loved her laugh. Her quick wit. Her personality. Her body. Her style and taste.

Which, if she were truly on the run from someone, why would she live so extravagantly? Maybe she didn't. She had a super nice vehicle, but it didn't really stand out where we lived. Otherwise, we lived in a cookie-cutter suburb, had your standard $300k condo, and she had a regular job.

Wait ... Her job had been a complete fabrication, so I'm not sure what she did all day.

What a mess.

Not just dealing with Elsie's disappearance, but my eggs.

I finally turned my attention back to the bowl of yellow and white. I tried to pick out the eggshells, but my tears would have to stay there. I wondered how they would taste. Sad? Bitter? Angry? Terrified? Probably a combination. Too many emotions. Without knowing exactly what had happened to Els, I wasn't sure how I should feel.

Ultimate Confusion. There we go.

The eggs would taste like ultimate confusion. It had a nice little ring to it.

I added a pinch of cheddar cheese that had stuck together—it was probably a little old—and a tablespoon of chili garlic sauce. That would have to do. There were some mushrooms that had gone bad, along with a slimy onion. I'd strongly considered both, probably spending five minutes weighing the pros and cons, but I opted against them.

Before going to bed, I looked outside my window, glancing across the street to Ally's house. I'd nearly forgotten about that mess amid everything else. Such a total shitstorm.

A man was standing outside. I couldn't tell who it was, all I could see was a red coat with a hood pulled tightly over his face.

He pulled the door open and went inside.

I panicked for a second, and I almost called the police. And then I remembered the time that she'd left the door open for me. I also quickly remembered that Kyle Bellamy wore a red jacket. That thought sickened me. Not so much because he was her teacher—that *should* have been enough, but because she was actually seeing him.

But what if it wasn't Kyle?

That thought punched me in the gut. What if it was an intruder? I debated calling 9-1-1.

Instead, I quickly pulled up Facebook to see if Ally was online. She was.

"Hey," I typed.

Instantly, three dots popped up next to her name.

"Wyd?"

So, she was okay. Not in any danger. But why would she be messaging me if she was hooking up with Kyle.

I collapsed on my bed, tossing my phone to the side. I hadn't realized just how exhausted I'd been. I fell asleep, blissfully ignorant to whatever was happening across the street.

Thirty-Four

MARK

I awoke the next morning, disoriented. I instantly knew that I'd been doing something before bed, something important.

That's right: Ally ... and Kyle.

Shit.

I checked my phone. New messages from Ally:

Okay then Mr. Wallace... Good night.

Something didn't seem right. It didn't sound like Ally. *When was the last time that she had actually called me Mr. Wallace?* I hadn't even considered that Kyle, or whoever was over there, could have sent me the message. Then again, maybe Ally was upset with me for blowing her off.

There's no way I would have done it, drunk or not. It would have been a huge mistake. Maybe calling me Mr. Wallace was her idea of formalizing things between us.

I wasn't about to try to get inside the mind of a teenage girl.

I exhaled and jumped from my bed.

I had enough going on. I couldn't worry about this. Elsie was gone and someone had threatened my sister. I guess they had threatened me, too, by putting that note outside of my hotel room. Someone had actually followed me there.

I peeked through my curtains, feeling the morning chill through the glass. It was colder than the morning after the poker game. I didn't see any action from Ally's house. I glanced back at my clock. It was a little past six. Ally usually left for her morning run about this time. Maybe she decided it was too cold.

If Kyle was still over, maybe she wouldn't. Maybe they were still tangled up in bed. My muscles tensed. It didn't matter, not to me, at least not personally. It was still wrong though.

He was her teacher.

After two minutes of watching, I forced myself to take a shower. I couldn't monitor Ally all morning. Some habits needed to be broken. Spying on an eighteen-year-old fell in that category, especially considering that Elsie was missing.

I let the water wash over me, cleansing my sins. *If only.* While in the shower, the thoughts came.

If only Elsie were still here, there's no way I would have even been tempted. I felt hurt and betrayed.

And Elsie doesn't want to have kids. Ally could.

I quickly pushed that thought aside.

The key would be to limit my drinking. All of my inhibitions and concept of right and wrong flew by the wayside. I guess it's that way for many people when they've had too many. There's a simple solution for that.

I needed more self-control. I was simply making excuses. Times like these are when the true character of a man is tested. When he's squeezed, what comes out?

I didn't like what was coming out of me. But it could have been worse. Hopefully, it wouldn't get worse. I needed to promise myself—to make a commitment—that I would not mess around with Ally or take another drink, or at least not more than a drink or two.

I needed to devote every resource and shred of energy to finding Elsie and whoever was responsible for leaving the note at my hotel room.

Hopefully, it wasn't too late.

Thirty-Five

ELSIE

After coming down from the mountain, I'd discovered that my classmate, Horace Qualls, had been murdered. I'd say that I couldn't believe it, but it was inevitable. I was sure that the bratva was trying to send a message. I just wondered how many more people would be drawn in. I'd hoped to avoid this.

I'd continued to keep a close eye on Mark's Facebook page. I had to. I didn't know what he might post, something about me? I couldn't let the wrong people see it. Not just for my safety, but for their own. I was sure that Horace, my former classmate, had only meant to help me.

When Mark had posted his desperate, loving plea, I broke

down. He was obviously shaken when I left, as I knew (hoped) he would be. I could literally feel his post, and I wanted to go back and comfort him. Unfortunately, I feared that would lead to his death.

Anyway, I couldn't let that post stay online. I'd taken such extreme measures to erase everything about me. Sydney. Elsie. Both. Most people wouldn't have had any idea who he was talking about, but I needed to make sure.

I reported his post for harassment. Initially, it was allowed to stay on the website, but I had to get further support from Facebook to explain how the man had been stalking me and had made the entire story up. I'd pleaded that I could be endangered if someone gave him a tip about my whereabouts.

That was enough. Maybe. Or maybe someone else intervened because they hadn't even responded to my messages. But one day I looked, and his post had disappeared.

In the end, it was to protect both of us. My only fear was who had seen the post before it was deleted. Maybe I should have been more proactive with Facebook. I wasn't sure what they could have done before he posted.

Too late now. Too late for Horace. Who knew how many more would die? I tried to do what I thought was best, but maybe I'd chosen poorly. I knew I'd been selfish, but all I'd ever wanted was a normal life.

Was that seriously too much to ask?

And if learning about Horace's death wasn't enough, it was about to get worse for me.

My phone rang. The energy was off. I didn't want to answer, but I knew that I had to.

After five rings, I finally answered. I pulled my phone slowly to my ear, bracing myself for the voice I'd hear—the edict, the threats. I didn't say a word.

"Sydney Porter," the man said, with a heavy accent. Not a question. He knew it was me. He knew I was there. I didn't say anything. I was still holding out hope—somewhere—that it wasn't them.

"Is Yuri," he said, firmly, without emotion. "You must answer for what you have done. We have you, Sydney Porter. After all of these years, we have you."

"What do you want?" I said, at least I must have. The sound came from my lips, but the words felt like they came from far away.

"You know what we want, Sydney."

From the time I'd left until now, I knew this day would come. When they would find me. I knew that I would never be safe. They had the resources, they had the men, and most importantly, they had every reason to keep searching. They had to find me.

I was a loose end and a killer.

I'd become so complacent. More than complacency, I think it was bitterness. Maybe some fatigue. I'd become so tired of living a fearful life. I'd like to say that I became courageous, but maybe I'd just been stupid. I hadn't thought things through enough. I didn't way back then, and I certainly hadn't lately.

Back then, I was too coked-out to register most of my thoughts—well, between that and the alcohol. Combine that with a little hatred and some fear, and the results wouldn't be good. Or they might even be horribly life-changing.

I'd have to go back to that night, relive it, but I wasn't ready to yet. I kept wanting to believe that I'd moved on from that. I barely even acknowledged that I was the same person.

I let down my guard, and that had been my undoing.

Thirty-Six

He walked back to his Tahoe after his meeting, intrigued by what he had just discovered. He hadn't been on this case long, but others had been trying to find some break for more than a decade. He wondered what the fallout would be. They needed to proceed with caution. He knew what they were dealing with: Desperation and the lust for vengeance. The two can be a terrifying combination.

He searched the area immediately surrounding his Tahoe. Nothing out of the ordinary. He opened the door and slid into the front seat.

After pulling away from the curb, he made his call.

"Agent Milhouse," the voice answered.

"I have confirmation. Target Sierra is Target November. I repeat Target Sierra is Target November.

There was a brief silence on the other end. "And you know this how?"

"I have documents and pictures, don't worry about that. Meet in fifteen at Target Bravo Whiskey Whiskey. Copy?"

"10-4. Over and out."

Thirty-Seven

MARK

Now that I had proof of Elsie's existence—and her real name, I could go to the authorities. *I could.* But I wasn't positive that it would be my best move. What if that would somehow endanger her? Was I selfish in wanting to find her? I didn't want my selfishness to somehow hurt her.

After returning from Chicago and learning of Horace's death, I felt like I needed to do something. I couldn't sit around and wait for more people to die. Thankfully, my sister was just fine when I'd called, but I still worried about her. That couldn't have been an empty threat, especially since Horace Qualls was now dead.

Armed with a *real* name and a face, I drove to the police station. I'd told reception that I needed to report a missing person. She had no idea who I was, but she told me that she'd get a detective to speak with me. She paged Brighton, and I sighed. I'd hoped that I could have spoken to someone else.

As soon as Brighton turned the corner, he shook his head.

"Shaw, meet me in the interrogation room. Mr. Wallace, come on back," he said, turning away from me.

"Let's make this quick."

I entered the room behind Shaw. It somehow seemed smaller than how they're usually depicted. Brighton and Shaw stood before me, just like the other time, except now I wasn't in the comfort of my apartment.

"Mr. Wallace, go ahead and have a seat," Brighton said. "Coffee?" he asked, somewhat rhetorically.

I declined and sat down. They took their seats across from me. The seat was cold. The walls closed in. I began to wonder if I'd made a mistake. I didn't think that I could somehow implicate myself, but I was worried. Maybe it came with being in an interrogation room, all of that residual energy from the countless nervous souls before me.

"Thanks for seeing me so quickly," I said, trying to start it off on the right track.

"It's a safe area, don't get too excited," Brighton said. "It's not like St. Louis," he said, swallowing hard. I sighed. He continued speaking. "We don't get many young girls left for dead along the side of the highway."

They knew.

And why wouldn't they? By now, they had definitely looked into my record. The entire incident flashed before my eyes as I tried to explain to them what had happened (leaving some of the details out). It's not like I owed them anything, but I didn't want to look ruthless.

The memory replayed in my mind:

I tried to avoid it, spinning the steering wheel desperately to the left, but it was too late. Water shot skyward around both cars. I wasn't sure how deep it was, but I lost control and hydroplaned. I tried to steer into the spin, but I could faintly make out a curve up ahead.

I tried to steady my car, to somehow keep it from sliding into the pole, but I'd lost all control. It really did happen in slow motion. There's something about those events that really does have a way of slowing down our perception of time. I didn't fully realize it until then. It just made the moment even more painful.

My airbag deployed, blasting me back into my seat.

The concussion of my car hitting the other car was nearly matched by other noises, at least in effect.

I could barely see around the now deflating airbag. The smell knocked me back. I tried to tear through the mess to get to safety.

I saw the body from the other car. A young woman, with so much life ahead of her. In a moment, she saw all of those future, precious moments erased from any potential reality.

One of my students. Riley Lawrence.

"Riley," I muttered. And then louder. "Riley!"

I think she tried to say something, but it came out as nothing more than a painful moan.

Blood poured from her forehead. I couldn't believe how quickly it seeped out of her.

Back in the present, I gave the officers an abbreviated version. I told them, "It had rained so hard; I could barely even see the road. And then there was this huge, deep puddle. I had no time to react. I hydroplaned, and I hit her."

The officers looked at each other. Shaw said, "But you left the scene, with alcohol in your blood. I honestly have no idea how the prosecution let you off. With nothing. The police over there don't know how either."

I felt sick. I hated recounting the incident, remembering how Riley had gone from lively to dying within seconds, and it was all because of me.

I had been silent, recounting those feelings that I'd had for her. I finally shook my head, looking down at the table. "My phone was dead. I was running to get her help. There weren't any houses around there. I ran so fast, faster than I thought possible. I'd been drinking, yeah, but I wasn't drunk. Not even close." I slapped the table. "Look, I know I should have been more careful, but I can guarantee that I'm not a ruthless killer."

"Why didn't you use her phone?" Shaw asked, critically.

"She had a passcode on it," I said. "Don't you think I would have tried that?" I tried to force a tear down my cheek for effect. "And I left St. Louis because of it. I just couldn't deal with the memories. I needed to get away and start fresh, even if it meant leaving all of my family and friends behind. Thought maybe I could go back later."

The officers might have softened, maybe as a result to my recitation of the event. Maybe they realized how much I had lost and how hard it had hit me. And now, I was dealing with another loss. Elsie was gone.

"Okay, okay, we'll switch gears and we will humor you. So, I assume you came here about …" He flipped through his notepad. "The *disappearance* of your live-in girlfriend, Elsie Morton? You told us that she left you, cut all contact, deleted you from Facebook, she changed her phone number, and that someone hacked into your phone to delete every picture of her. Does that sum it up?"

I tried to mentally switch gears. It was hard. I debated how to proceed. I was going to sound crazy, crazier than the last time I'd called them.

I took a deep breath. They waited.

I exhaled and said, "Her name isn't Elsie Morton." They exchanged glances. I was thankful that they didn't immediately cut me off. I continued. "Elsie's name is actually Sydney Porter. And look, I know this sounds insane, but I can't find anything about her after she graduated high school. No Facebook. Nothing on Google. Nothing. It's like she doesn't exist."

Brighton started to speak—it wasn't going to be good, so I cut him off. "I have her yearbook. I have pictures of her. She was an all-state athlete. She placed in two different sports. After

I posted about her disappearance on Facebook, one of her old classmates contacted me. That person is now dead. His name was Horace Qualls."

Brighton shifted, narrowing his eyes. "He was murdered downtown a few days ago, and we had no leads." He leaned closer, like he was trying to keep Shaw from hearing him. Coffee was thick on his breath.

I already knew what was coming, but it was ludicrous to even consider. There was no way I could have murdered Horace Qualls. I'd been in Chicago at the time of his death, halfway across the country. It would be easy for them to verify that it couldn't have been me.

He continued. "Are you saying that you had contact with Horace Qualls in the days leading up to his death?

"Have you struck again?"

Thirty-Eight

The six men were back in the war room. Circumstances had changed since their last meeting, held only a few short days before. Yuri strongly doubted that this new information was not known before. Just as he had suspected, not everything had been disclosed during their phone conversation.

This time, Yuri stood at the window, peering out over Lake Michigan. It all looked so peaceful. The lake and the city below. All of the chaos was blocked by the window. It didn't hurt that they were also forty-plus stories above ground level.

Yuri wasn't opposed to chaos though, as long as it served a purpose. He would have preferred to live without it, but he had found that chaos could be a motivating force in closing deals. It had an effect on someone's propensity to see things his way.

He thought of his son, how he had been robbed of his life, taken from his world without so much as a goodbye. Yuri remembered seeing the pictures. He had also watched the video from inside the home, forever imprinting that movie in his head.

He swore that he would exact vengeance, no matter what it took. He had the men to do it. Many were too young to remember, not much older than his precious granddaughter, but they wouldn't hesitate to act to protect the bratva.

One of the men came up to his right side, not saying anything, but also looking out over the water, seemingly trying to find what Yuri was looking at, but he wasn't going to find it.

Although Yuri's eyes were open and he was looking outside the window, he was deep in his mind, planning out exactly how he was going to kill Sydney Porter and Mark Wallace.

Thirty-Nine

ELSIE

After speaking with Yuri, Elsie mentally replayed the incident that caused Sydney Porter to run.

The actual murder (or assassination) of Sergei Kalishav was quick and easy. That had been well-planned and executed. Sydney drugged his drink, just as Elsie Morton would later do to Mark Wallace. Except, this time, she wasn't being protective of the man.

After Sergei dozed off, Elsie exited the bedroom momentarily. She replayed everything in her head, how she had lost Julia. How she had watched her dying there on the floor, restrained by the bratva from trying to call for help. Because of

Sergei she lost her best friend and their future together. He had robbed them of so much.

She also considered what the ramifications would be. She knew that the bratva would come after her in some way. She was also still young. She was still somewhat impulsive, but she'd probably always be more impulsive than most.

This was her chance though, and she'd already taken the steps to make this possible. The money was tucked away. She knew where she needed to run. She'd be fine. She could start fresh somewhere. And after a while, maybe it would blow over and she could return to her family and friends.

She came back into the room with a gun. Sergei was sleeping on his side, looking away from her. She knew he was out, though. She'd already tested him.

She felt no emotion for Sergei as she leaned over the bed and placed a pillow against the back of his head.

He didn't stir.

She guided the gun deep into the pillow, the barrel close to his head. She took a deep breath and pulled the trigger.

Sergei Kalishav died instantly.

Sydney's kill count was now one. There would be several more to follow.

Forty

MARK

I'd asked for a lawyer. I had to. I was afraid that I'd say something else that sounded bad. I honestly hadn't even considered that I could have been pulled into Horace's death. Apparently, Horace hadn't called me from his real phone number, so they hadn't had previous knowledge that he had called me.

Likewise, nobody had recognized us sitting together at the Starbucks, even though a barista did remember seeing him there. She couldn't begin to identify me at the time.

Now, she probably could.

It didn't matter at this point though. They already knew that I had spoken with him.

They had terminated the interview, saying that I wasn't under arrest and had never had any obligation to answer any of their questions.

I had a feeling it would come though. Maybe. Hopefully, my lawyer would be able to help me with that. I'd also realized that I'd only *learned* of Horace's death while in Chicago. He may have been murdered while I was still in Colorado.

Within an hour of leaving the police station, I found myself in a boutique Denver law firm. They were all criminal defense attorneys. I was led into an office by a lithe secretary with black-rimmed glasses and a pencil skirt.

"Anything to drink?" she asked.

"No thanks," I said. Her smile lingered on me before she turned back down the hall.

"Come in, have a seat."

I readjusted to the office. A large desk with a wall of diplomas and certificates. Everything was wooden. I caught a whiff of whiskey and cigars.

My attorney, Chase Bloom, came around the desk to shake my hand. He was a head shorter than me, but he carried himself like he was a head taller. Maybe it was his flowing mane.

He cut right to the chase and had me explain everything. After just a moment's pause, he said, "Anything they have against you is circumstantial. You spoke with this man before his death, so-fucking-what? That happens. He probably also talked to dozens of other people that week. That doesn't mean shit."

I nodded along with the attorney, enjoying his enthusiasm.

"I honestly wouldn't worry too much about that," he said. "If anything happens, they'll try to bring you in for questioning. They'll want to know more about the subject matter of your conversation. Even if they can't pin the murder on you, they're still investigating a homicide, and they'll want answers."

"So, do I wait for them to call me?"

"You're definitely not going to drive down there. Is that what you were thinking? Don't talk to them."

I thought about this. "But if I explained what we talked about, maybe they would take Elsie's disappearance seriously. It might be my only way to have them investigate. Plus, wouldn't I look guilty if I didn't talk to them?"

"Yes and no," Bloom said. "They still wouldn't have *near* enough evidence, standing alone, to arrest you for anything. Once again, you merely talked to the fucking guy. That's it. Now, if they knew the content of this conversation. If they knew that he directed you back to Chicago because he knew Elsie, and if they can somehow connect him to Elsie—or Sydney—whoever, then who knows what they might piece together." He let out a long rush of air. "This is some crazy shit, man."

"You're telling me."

"Tell me more about your girlfriend. We do have some resources where we can track people down—witnesses, clients, debtors. Have you spoken to a private investigator? I have one of the best on retainer. I always tell people that I have the best dick around." I snorted, but he didn't miss a beat. "Of course, you'd also have to put me on retainer."

He tapped his fingers on the desk.

"I honestly hadn't even thought of a PI. Do you think that would help?"

He grinned slightly. "Look, I might be a little biased. I can't guarantee that we would get you any results, but yes, like I said, my dick is good. If anyone could track her down and learn more about her past, it's this guy. For this specifically, I would ask for a retainer of five thousand. Keep in mind, a decent chunk of this would go to him. I would be facilitating though, providing my legal expertise as we go. And if you desire representation in a potential criminal case, I'd need an additional retainer of ten thousand. Mark, I honestly don't see that happening though. I don't think they'll be able to charge you with shit. And I'm always more than willing to provide further guidance at my hourly rate of four hundred per hour, without any retainer."

I had to catch my breath. If I needed to pay both retainers, that would have been one-third of a year's salary. Once again, I was thankful that I had money saved up. I also realized that even fifteen thousand was cheaper than most new cars. This was my life—and potentially, Elsie's—at stake. It was definitely more than worth it.

"I can pay the five thousand," I said. "Just let me switch some money over to my account. Maybe in two days?"

"Perfect," he said. "On your way out, my secretary will have a contract for you to sign. And Mark, try to get some sleep. You look like shit, bro."

Forty-One

ELSIE

After shooting Sergei, Sydney didn't even make it off the compound before she was taken into custody. The Feds had been monitoring a planned assassination attempt on Sergei. They hadn't suspected Sydney, but instead, they thought that she had witnessed his death.

She wasn't going to argue with them.

They took her to a safe house. They claimed that she was in protective custody—to protect her from the bratva. She wondered if they would ultimately try to charge her with Sergei's murder—once they figured out the truth. Even though she was paying him back for killing Julia, deep down, she knew it wasn't the right way to do it. Plus, there was no way that it would ever bring Julia back.

Two federal Marshals had been entrusted with guarding Sydney Porter. Their orders had come directly from the Deputy Director of the U.S. Department of Justice.

Other agencies were also involved: FBI, CIA, Chicago Police Department. It was messy business when the Kalishav bratva was involved.

Two Marshals watched over Sydney at the safe house. One man, one woman. The man was Trent Swinton. Tall, close to six-foot-five. He was built like the Sears Tower. In fact, that had been his nickname growing up. *Sears Tower.* His black hair, olive skin, and piercing brown eyes topped it off. Despite his imposing size, he had a large heart. He adored his wife and his two young children.

Wendy Reich was his partner, had been for the last eleven months. She had a chip on her shoulder, a full foot shorter than her partner (and with less testosterone, but not much), but she made up for any perceived deficiency with her bulldog determination. And her brilliance.

In a short hour, two Marshals would arrive to relieve them of their post.

Sydney was in the next room. They thought she had been sleeping, but she was listening intently, waiting for the exchange. Call it a hunch, but she had a feeling that it wasn't going to be a smooth transfer of power. It was something she had heard the night before, something she wasn't supposed to hear.

She'd had interactions with Marshal Swinton. She liked him. Not Reich, though. She was ice cold. And why wouldn't she be? She felt instinctively threatened by the more attractive, younger woman. At least that's what Sydney had told herself. Sydney didn't even consider how that script could possibly flip someday.

Maybe Reich saw Sydney for what she really was. Sydney could have claimed that she was seeking retribution for her friend's death, but she still killed a man after he fell asleep. She had that in her.

It's possible that the drugs, alcohol, and seldom having a clear head impaired her judgment a little. She could also blame some of her choices on perfectionist parents who pushed her to succeed at everything, but millions of kids go through the same thing without taking up the hobbies of cocaine and murder.

Sydney had nobody to blame but herself. Deep down, she knew that, even if others tried to make excuses for her. She was far from a Disney princess, but she always did what she felt was the right thing.

Later that afternoon, Sydney overheard Marshal Swinton recite his plans for the evening. He was kicked back in his chair with his feet on the table. He said, "I'm ready to get out of this house, go home, see the wife and kids, fire up the grill, and hang out by the pool."

"Lucky," Reich said. "That sounds awesome." Reich had never married and didn't have any kids. At this point, she feared that she was too old.

The exchange was scheduled for six. In the summer months,

there was still plenty of daylight. However, the replacements had called to say that they'd hit a bit of a snag. Flat tire. Swinton and Reich had no reason to suspect anything. They recognized the voice of the man who called, and the two Marshals were already back on the road. They'd simply be an hour late.

What they didn't know was that anyone could be bought. There hadn't been a flat tire, but the two Marshals were making another exchange at that time, trading their vehicle and uniforms for cash. Lots of it. They would be out of the country before any news of the compromise.

The two Marshals heard the car pull up. It approached the drive normally. Nothing erratic to give them away. The replacements parked, opened and shut their doors, and approached the house. Nothing out of the ordinary.

Swinton had just told a knock-knock joke involving dogs that had Reich rolling. But in less than fifteen seconds, Swinton and Reich would go from laughing and smiling to dead.

The two men blasted into the room, guns blazing. The first shot picked Swinton up off his chair, discarding what was left of him into the opposite side of the kitchen.

Reich had tried to pull her weapon, but she was fileted by a cascade of shotgun pellets. She was ripped apart.

"We locate the target and kill her," one man said to the other.

From upstairs, Sydney heard the gunshots thundering through the house. She thought it might collapse. She thought she'd be more scared, but she really wasn't. All of her senses were heightened. She couldn't freeze. If she did, she would die.

Even if she didn't, the odds were still stacked against her. There were two of them against her. They also surely had more experience than she did.

How was she going to survive?

She heard the men talking in low tones below her, scouring the lower-level rooms. There weren't many rooms in the house, nowhere to hide. Soon, they would climb the stairs and find her. She needed to somehow gain an advantage.

Picking them off one at a time was her best bet. She needed to funnel them to her. Even then, she would have to be perfect with her shots. And quick.

Thankfully, she had been observant. She knew this house better than they did. She doubted that the two men had ever been inside. They didn't know that there was another set of stairs that she was now—carefully—descending.

The steps were carpeted, so that helped muffle any noise that she might have made. She'd left herself exposed while going down, but they were still a couple of rooms away from reaching the partially hidden staircase.

She could hear their thundering footfalls. They clearly weren't worried about her or giving away their location. They probably thought they had her cornered in one of the rooms.

Before she turned into the kitchen, she could smell it. The lingering sulfur mixed with death. Acrid and uncomfortable. She had killed Sergei only a few days before, but this was somehow worse. Maybe because the two Marshals had sacrificed their lives trying to protect her after she had murdered a man.

She couldn't wait around anymore. The men were getting closer to the steps. Would they come down together or split up, with one taking the other set of stairs?

It didn't matter, she'd be ready.

Sydney entered the kitchen and almost gasped. She wanted to cry, but she couldn't. It was like nothing she had ever seen. In the movies, yes, but this was different. Every other sense was engaged in a cacophony of chaos and loss.

She eased over to Swinton, knowing that he wouldn't have that barbecue with his family. Elsie wondered how they would ever move on. She couldn't consider that now, though, she didn't have the time or else her parents would be mourning her.

Swinton had barely drawn his revolver. It was slightly out of its holster, but his hand had dropped down to his side.

Sydney carefully removed her pistol. It was loaded and the safety was off. She had researched guns when she was planning to take out Sergei, when she was debating the best way to effectuate her plan.

She looked at the other Marshal, or what was left of her. She nearly gagged and lost it.

Footsteps erupted on the stairs behind her. She couldn't tell if it was one set or two, but they were moving.

She needed to act fast. She leaned over Reich, debating on whether she should grab her gun. She reasoned that she probably had enough and it wasn't worth it. It would slow her down. She needed both arms to properly aim, anyway. She wasn't so strong and needed more support.

She tiptoed past Reich and into the room where they had held her. It had been turned upside down in a frantic search. The mattress thrown against the wall. The clothes in the closet scattered everywhere.

The men hit the bottom of the stairs. No, just one man. Right after the first man descended the stairs behind her, she heard the other man come down the other set. They would have come at her from both sides. She'd be in the bedroom now though. If she had known they would have come down one-by-one, she could have waited at the bottom of one set of stairs and taken them out individually.

But had they come down together, she would have been dead. There was no way to win.

They both crept toward her, closing in. It became quiet.

Too quiet.

"She took a gun." The voice was low, right on the other side of the wall. That meant that the other guy was close enough to hear. Close to entering the room.

Sydney couldn't afford to panic. She needed to keep her wits about her. She briefly considered her options. She'd almost have to pick them off as they entered the room.

If only there was some way to distract them.

She didn't have time to think of a plan, the first man neared the doorway and she acted instinctively. She'd had a pen in her pocket. She tossed it against the far end of the room. It was just enough of a distraction for the man to turn that way when he entered the room.

Sydney shot him in the forehead and directly through his brain. She could hardly believe that she had hit him.

The force flung him into the discarded mattress, and he crumpled to the floor.

She rocked backward from the force of the gun, but she was able to steady herself. That was important since the next man was right behind the other, taking dead aim. She couldn't even think. Once again, she just had to react and take the shot.

She wasn't quite as lucky when the next man barged into the room. The first shot hit his shoulder. Thankfully, it was the arm that held the gun. His arm flung backward, the gun slipping from his grasp. She thought he would have to lean down to pick it up, but he spun back toward her and quickly removed another pistol from his shoulder holster. He held it toward her, steadying his aim, about to pull the trigger and end her life.

She snapped out of her daze just soon enough to send another bullet through his chest. It had shaken him enough to momentarily halt his progress, but he kept coming. He raised his arm one more time.

It would be the last time.

Sydney shot him in the face. He fell down, his head crashing into the floor, just to her left, sending teeth and blood flying around her.

She couldn't scream. She couldn't do anything. She was frozen. Elsie briefly surveyed the carnage, but she knew that she needed to leave. She honestly thought she might be able to smooth things over with the Feds. They surely knew what had happened, but she was more worried about the bratva.

If they were able to successfully infiltrate the safehouse, would she ever be safe? The feds could promise her that she would be taken care of, new identity, whatever it took, but she feared that the bratva would always find her.

And once again, if the feds found out the specifics about Sergei's death, they might lock her away for life. Sydney made the decision that would shape the rest of her life …

She took off running into the humid Chicago night.

Forty-Two

MARK

After making it back home, I looked at myself in the mirror. Bloom was right, I looked like crap. The stress was taking its toll. Losing my job, losing Elsie, the bratva coming after me, my sister being threatened, waiting to be arrested for having sex with a student, reliving the night that Riley died.

Brutal, but most of it was ultimately self-inflicted. I'd still be working if not for Ally.

Anyway, a hot, steamy shower is supposed to be a cure-all. Hungover? Take a hot shower. Exhausting workout? Shower. Girlfriend disappear with all of her belongings, including the pictures in your phone? A shower couldn't hurt. Russian bratva threatening your family? Shower. It probably won't help much, but it couldn't hurt. That was reassuring.

After Elsie's disappearance, stepping into the shower was a little different. Bumping into bottles and bottles of shit was no longer an issue. My shampoo and conditioner were always stored on the far side of the shower. We had a shower caddy hanging over the showerhead, but it was overflowing. Razors, shaving cream, face wash, a few bottles I didn't recognize.

I'd never appreciated it before, but now I missed it.

I missed all of it.

My phone was flashing from the edge of our bed—*my* bed. That flashing green light that indicated a text message, Facebook message, or a voicemail. There didn't seem to be any distinguishing characteristic between the three, maybe the Facebook notifications blinked slightly more rapidly. I don't know.

The notification could have been for any one of the three. Not sure which I wanted or feared the most. A voicemail could be from anyone, so, yeah, I probably didn't want one of those.

Before checking, I finished drying off, threw my towel on the floor and put on a pair of boxer briefs and basketball shorts.

Had to look presentable.

I sat down on the bed and picked up my phone; Elsie used to smile back at me. My background picture had been one that I had taken of her in Breck, posing at the top of Peak 10.

But now? Nothing. Just a black filler. I suppose I could have put a picture of Ally on there.

Yeah, right.

My eyes flipped to the notification bar.

Voicemail. Shit.

Not from a saved number, either. As much as I didn't want to listen to it. Maybe it was news regarding Elsie's whereabouts.

Mr. Wallace, this is Christina from Attorney Chase Bloom's office. I was just calling to see when you would be able to drop off payment at our office. Attorney Bloom is eager to get your case started. Thank you and have a great day.

She left the office's number and wished me well.

I'm sure he was eager to get the case started and eager to get his payday.

I knew that I needed to pay him. *$5,000*. And that was just the beginning. I wondered how much more I'd have to pay, especially if I had to fight criminal charges.

At this point, did I even want to track Elsie down?

I would have loved to just get on with my life, but after what had happened to Horace and the ominous note about my sister? I couldn't really just keep living my life as usual, pretending that everything was perfect. And, I really did miss her. My feelings seemed to grow stronger in her absence. It's always funny how that works.

I went ahead and withdrew money from my checking account and paid Bloom. I caught myself wondering what his *dick* actually charged per hour. Maybe I could have saved a little money by cutting out the middle man.

Oh well. I could probably use more legal advice, anyway. I'll probably need it.

And maybe I'll get expedited or better service from the P.I. since his being retained by my lawyer.

It didn't really matter.

I met with Bloom back in his office, hoping that this would somehow be worth it. I didn't know what the P.I. would be able to find, but it was surely worth a shot.

"How long does it usually take?" I asked Bloom before leaving his office.

"It all depends." He steepled his fingers on his desk. "I do have some clout, so I pushed this along. That's part of the reason why you come to me and not him." *Knew it.* "But hell, it might take a few days, it might take two weeks. If he needs to visit Chicago or conduct more thorough research, I hope you realize that you might have to pay more. Is that okay?"

I swallowed hard. It felt like I'd just stepped into a steam bath. "How much more?"

He looked annoyed by the question. "Christ, man, it could be several thousand more. You have our hourly charges. Plus, a flight to Chicago can be several hundred without buying an advanced ticket. Hotel could be a few hundred for a few nights. Maybe a trail leads to Memphis or Raleigh. And who knows? We might not even hit the retainer amount."

I'm not naïve enough to believe that. I was relieved though. For some reason, traveling across the country always seems more expensive than it really is.

"Tell you what," Bloom said. "I don't always do this, but when you hit the retainer amount, I'll let you know. I'll also let you know where he stands in his investigation at that time, and then you can decide whether or not you want to proceed. Fair enough?"

I agreed and left.

Money should have been the least of my concerns. If the P.I. could figure something out—if he could keep my family safe, it would be worth everything. I continued to wonder how Elsie played into all of this, if she was a victim or the perp.

Forty-Three

ELSIE

It was always hard to relive everything. I usually tried not to think about what had happened. My life had taken a drastically different course after I killed Sergei.

What would Mark think if he knew the truth? My crazy life between Sydney and Elsie, and all of the other names that I'd used—the different faces that I wore. The times that I made desperate exchanges to survive or to at least make life more comfortable on the road.

I didn't need to share everything with him, but I would try to fill in some of the gaps. I swore it to myself. As long as we both survived this, I'd be honest with him. I'd tried to do everything for his protection. For *our* protection.

There was basically a decade between Chicago and the mountains outside of Leadville. I wish I'd known about the mountains earlier in my journey. It would have made life far less stressful. In the summer, anyway. The winter might have been tricky. It gets brutally cold in the mountains.

Thankfully, I'd walked away with plenty of money. At least three hundred thousand. It sounds like a lot, but after ten years, it can get stretched thin if you're not smart. I'd been very smart though. I'd even invested some through a friend. When you do that, you can make it go a long way.

Shortly after leaving Chicago, I'd put at least twenty-five thousand into buying and renovating a sleeper van. I installed a fridge, a reliable power source, a more comfortable bed, and security reinforcements. It had been a decent chunk of my reserves, but it would also double as my lodging for the foreseeable future.

I couldn't risk anything. I knew the bratva would be after me, but I also feared that the federal government might also be looking for me. Did they know that the Marshals had been compromised or did they think that I killed all four of them? Did they figure out what had actually happened to Sergei?

I thought they'd have some way of checking. Ballistics? They'd know that I couldn't have killed them all because my gun wouldn't be a match to the others.

Anyway, I'd bought the van outside of Milwaukee during the

early morning following the shootout. Afterward, I'd shot north. It was summer, thankfully. I drove all the way to the upper peninsula of Michigan and stayed there for a while. I even picked up some work as a bartender, just to keep money coming in.

That was my basic operation as I moved southwest over the years. That first winter, I found myself in the Ozarks. I'd moved further south into Oklahoma and then to Texas because even Missouri gets damn cold.

I spent a lot of time in west Texas. It's so wide open and desolate. Even the larger cities, Amarillo and Lubbock, seem like small towns, especially compared to Chicago.

I felt safe. Nobody ever really questioned me. I was also able to secure sturdier identification. I was amazed by how cheap someone can buy a new identity on the black market. It's still incredibly illegal, but anyone can do it. If you need to.

I'd definitely needed to.

I spent years circling around West Texas and New Mexico before easing into Colorado one summer. That was the summer that I met Mark and everything changed.

It had been so long, and I was so tired of running. I missed real life. I wanted to take the chance for all of that. To me, it was worth risking. At some point, are you even living if you're constantly running scared and hiding? If you're constantly bouncing around? How much is life really worth living? There is something powerful about having some stability and putting down roots. Introducing more order into our lives often reduces chaos and anxiety.

That's not to say that I hadn't had some fun while bounding around the country in my van. I'd met some great friends and had some romances, but everything was so brief and fleeting. I could never add anyone on Facebook or keep in contact. I'd always had to watch my back.

Romances could never turn into anything more. After a while, it all becomes so empty and soulless. I yearned for a real relationship, and I desperately wanted a family. I also wanted to find a steadier, more fulfilling job. I enjoyed bartending, but I'd also been going to school to be a doctor.

I think that's why I told Mark that I worked at Arapahoe Memorial. I couldn't tell him that I was a doctor though, that would be a little too hard to verify if he ever looked into it—for whatever reason. But I longed for that future that I'd lost on that Chicago summer night.

I needed to somehow find a semblance of that.

And one night, Mark just happened to be there.

The band was playing. He had that rugged yet sophisticated look. He wasn't trying too hard, either. From the moment I met him, I knew he was smart and stable. Exactly what I needed at that point in my life. That's not to say that it was completely smooth. I know I made things difficult by my extreme apprehension about letting my guard down and believing that I could have something real with someone like Mark. I'd definitely tried to self-sabotage myself.

Mark had grown up near St. Louis and moved to Colorado to be in the mountains. I admired his courage to leave everything behind. I felt like I could relate to him, even though I'd been forced to move. He'd never really given me a solid reason for moving other than just wanting to start fresh somewhere.

Maybe he'd also had his reasons, but I honestly didn't care about his past. Not at all. I only cared about who he was now.

Forty-Four

MARK

My attorney had called to let me know that the P.I. had found something. "Just the tip, not full penetration, but it's going to be a rough fuck," he had said. His humor seemed ill-timed, but it also reminded me that maybe better times were ahead. Either way, at least he had found something ... *Quickly.*

Our conversation led me to a small, rundown park, just a few miles from our apartment. One of those parks where the swings were hanging from one chain, and it looked like the slide might collapse if you took a chance. *Adventure.*

There was a little impound yard that was surrounded by a chain-link fence. I was now looking at Elsie's abandoned Infiniti SUV, surrounded by an old Chevy Lumina and a Ford Focus.

"Find anything?" I asked the investigator. He wasn't quite what I expected, not sure why. I pictured a stone-faced beefcake, but this guy could have passed for a computer tech.

"I have," he said, widening his eyes, his voice higher than I'd imagined. "This is her vehicle, correct? Plates the same? Distinguishing little dent on the back fender, correct?"

"Yeah," I said. "It's definitely hers. I remembered the license plate. It wasn't a vanity plate, but I'd seen it every day. It's easy for that to imprint in your brain.

"Well, it's not her car," he said, tossing a large envelope into the air and toward my face.

I caught it and raised my eyebrows. "What do you mean, it's not hers? She drove it every day."

"Check it out and see for yourself," he said, with his hands on his hips. He sniffled. "This damn cold air. I'm so ready for summer."

My fingers traced the opening of the envelope. It was more like a small folder—what the dealerships put the paperwork in when you buy a car.

I took out the registration and title. I squinted, sure that there had been a malfunction somewhere between my eyes and brain. Otherwise, this was beyond comprehension.

Now, I could add a new name to add to the mix …

Elsie Morton, Sydney Porter, and *Josiah Wilkins.*

I blinked rapidly, simply staring at the name, unable to say anything. I couldn't even begin to process this information.

Josiah Wilkins?

I flashed my eyes back to the P.I., mouth agape, begging him to explain what I'd just seen.

He grinned slightly, shaking his head. "You're in some crazy shit, aren't you, buddy?"

I looked at the name again, willing it to magically change back to Elsie or Sydney. Yes, Elsie *or* Sydney. At least that would simplify things a little bit. Dealing with two names was crazy enough, but I didn't even know how to react to this.

"Now, brace yourself because it gets worse," he said.

"Go on," I said, not sure what could rock me at this point.

"You know the guy who died, Horace Qualls?"

"Sure," I said. "I met with him a few days before."

"Guess where they found his body."

I simply raised my eyebrows and shrugged.

"In Elsie's Infiniti." He read off her plate numbers. "Those are her plates, right? Those are the numbers you gave me."

I froze, letting his proclamation wash over me. My skin must have turned five shades lighter, and it had already been ashen.

He continued. "The Infiniti was found at the address they gave on the news, but they didn't share the additional information. The Infiniti is being kept as evidence. One of the officers owed me a favor, so he's letting me take a peek at it. Anyway, I don't know if they've swept it for prints yet, but I'm sure they will. And when they do, they'll find Elsie's—sorry, Sydney's prints all over the vehicle. I'd say to get her a great attorney, but you already have Bloom. Plus, they can't arrest a ghost."

My head was spinning. Elsie surely couldn't have been responsible for killing Horace. What motive would she have had? Maybe she didn't want me or anyone else digging into her past. Had she been completely innocent?

"I have a theory," he said, likely concluding that I was too shook to say anything. "She bought this off the books. You said that she had money, right?"

"Right." I nodded, closing my eyes, completely shutting out the world around me.

"So, she buys this. Nothing can be traced to her. Either name. She has nothing in her name, right? It also makes for a quick getaway. No questions asked if anyone finds the vehicle. But people have seen her driving this. Maybe not many, but some. She discards it, and she probably find another car. Something that she had no previous connection to, that absolutely no one can trace."

I exhaled loudly. "Makes sense."

He continued. "The problem I have with Elsie doing this is, why would she leave Horace's body in her own vehicle? Right?"

"Right," I said, feeling better, but the P.I. continued. "But it's not her vehicle. It's not registered to her. It's registered to a man named, Josiah Wilkins, remember?"

I shook my head. "Wow."

"So, she could have very well done this, stashed Horace's body in this vehicle and fled. I still find it unlikely though."

The P.I. took out a handkerchief and blew his nose, then continued. "Something tells me that this is a message from the

Kalishav bratva. They were probably following her, then swooped in on the Infiniti when she transferred vehicles. But then again, if they had been following her, they would have just taken her. So, who knows?"

I sure didn't. It felt like the more I discovered, the less I knew about Elsie and what had happened.

Forty-Five

ELSIE

I thought back to when I'd left Mark.

Completely vanishing would have been impossible without proper planning. I couldn't lug all of my things out of the house in one afternoon. I couldn't be sure how much time I would have the next day, so I did a lot of my work the night before.

Lying in bed with Mark that night nearly threw me off course. His strong arms around me, his body pressed against mine. But I couldn't turn back, he had left me no choice.

I'd tested him with a little bump and grind to see if the drugs had taken effect. He was generally unresponsive. And he expressly said that he was too tired to have sex. It was all going according to my plan.

His breathing continued to slow, then he began to snore. Not loudly, but a cute little rumble. Enough so that I knew he was out.

But I decided to wait an hour or so, just to make sure he was completely gone. Drugging him had been the easy part, slipping the white powder into his final beer at dinner.

Yeah, I felt guilty doing it, but it was a minor sin—compared to what I had done, and what I was about to do.

Part of me wondered if it might be better just to kill him now. It might save both of us pain and suffering later. I could have made it as painless as possible for him.

A truck passed below, interrupting my thoughts. The truck was loud, but Mark didn't stir. I turned to face him, studying his face. He was dead to the world; a little slobber was running down the corner of his lips.

Cute.

I grinned, but I didn't make a sound. He looked so innocent when he was asleep … and drugged.

I turned back toward him. I had the urge to kiss his forehead, so I did. Softly. My lips pressed against the slight crease above his eyes. I lingered for a moment, savoring the saltiness. I only ended the kiss when I feared that a teardrop might run down my cheek and onto his face. Surely, that would have woken him.

The clock showed *2:14.*

Time to move, in many ways. I turned away from Mark, looking over my shoulder to once again make sure that he wasn't waking up.

Nothing, just another snore. This one was a little louder. Hopefully that meant that he was sleeping more deeply.

I'd already taken some of my things to my Infiniti. It was amazing how much I could thin the closet without Mark noticing. Same thing regarding my bathroom supplies. If he would have asked about the thinned closet, I would have just told him that I'd taken clothes to Goodwill.

Believable enough.

With Mark dead to the world, I went to work on his phone, deleting any trace of me. I then took a few more things outside. I'd come back after he left for work to erase everything, but I needed to get a head start.

I stayed away in the morning. For all he knew, I had simply gone to work at Arapahoe Memorial. That was a nice cover. I waited an hour or two after he normally left, and then I drove back to our place.

All of my clothes—haphazardly tossed in three suitcases, my bathroom items tossed in a large bag, and I took a couple of the pictures of us I'd placed in the apartment.

It was tempting to leave something behind, but I couldn't risk it. I'd even scoured the apartment for bobby pins and shed hair while Mark was at work the day before.

Disappear without a trace. I'd had practice. I knew how to cover my ass.

Forty-Six

MARK

I was driving home after meeting with the investigator. Too many thoughts were bouncing around my head. I wanted to think that the bratva had killed Horace—not Elsie, but then that left another nasty alternative. Had they already tracked her down and killed her? Were they sending a message that they had her?

Turning on to Walker Street, I could already sense that something bad was going to happen. I'm not sure how that was possible, maybe some kind of premonition or sixth sense. A warning call from God. I honestly didn't know, but I felt it, as thick as the humidity on a summer day back in St. Louis.

Even though it was cold outside, I felt the same suffocation. *It was about to get worse.*

I saw a man standing on the sidewalk, a few houses further down the street than mine. He was looking at my apartment building. Even from my distance, he looked huge, dressed in dark colors.

I would circle the block, see if he was gone by the time I came back. Once I accelerated, he finally turned in my direction. He was stone-faced, showing absolutely no recognition or response to my passing. I'd say he looked Russian or Eastern European, but that's probably just because that's what I was expecting. He had a face full of stubble and both of his ears were pierced with diamond studs. Dark eyes. Other than that, nothing distinguishable. No face tattoos or anything. He honestly looked like a regular guy … One who was standing near my house days after my girlfriend went missing and after my sister essentially received a death threat.

Other than that, just a regular guy …

I made a right turn at the end of the street and then another. I realized that I was driving by the spot where I'd run into Ally. Things had been far less complicated then, and they were still crazy at that point. I wondered how much more was going to change in the coming days.

I hoped my sister was okay. And Ethan and Ella.

I took a deep breath as I made my third right turn. One more, and I'd be back on my street.

Making the fourth turn, I braced myself.

Nothing. No one. The man had vanished.

I couldn't remember if there had been a random car parked along the street or in another driveway. I'd been too focused on the man.

I exhaled, but only slightly. I didn't think I had a neighbor who looked like that, but I honestly seldom paid attention to *most* of my neighbors.

I made my pivot and parked along the curb, directly behind where Elsie's Infiniti should have been.

The wind picked up, carrying a discarded paper cup down the street. I watched as it flew into the intersection and was crushed by a passing truck.

Still distracted, I opened my car door and stepped outside. It was chilly but not too bad. I walked around the backside of my car, turning to my apartment.

I froze.

The man was standing in front of my door, staring me down. He wasn't more than twenty feet away.

He took four large steps forward and stopped. He had nearly bridged the gap between us. He looked at me, steaming. I hadn't realized how large he was.

I was frozen in place. I just stared.

"Two days," he said, flashing a peace sign. "You have two days to produce Elsie."

And with that, he charged right at me.

I didn't have time to react.

I was able to find some traction and take off running down

the sidewalk. I braced for impact. He had already built up speed. He would surely catch me and tackle me to the ground.

I'd already taken several steps, but I didn't hear anyone behind me. I glanced back, still expecting him to be on my heels, but he had apparently taken off in the opposite direction. I watched as he disappeared around the block.

I fell to the sidewalk, barely registering the impact. I was shaking, knowing that this wasn't good. Not for me. Not for Elsie. Not for my sister. Not for anyone.

You have two days to produce Elsie.

What did that even mean? How was I supposed to find her?

I didn't want to think what would happen if I didn't produce her. Is that when they would go after my sister? Perhaps they would torture me for information.

I also thought of the Infiniti. If they had actually taken her and planted Horace inside her car as some kind of message, then they obviously wouldn't need me to produce her. Unless someone else had gotten to her first.

I honestly didn't know what to think. It was too overwhelming. All I knew for sure was that I had two days to produce her, and I had no idea where to begin.

Forty-Seven

MARK

Bloom's secretary had called to set an appointment later in the day. I'd tried asking her if the P.I. had found anything new, but she claimed that she had no idea. She said that I'd have to wait to speak to the attorney.

It must have been juicy if he went ahead and set an appointment the same day. I became fearful of what I might discover, then again, I didn't think it could be any worse than anything else that had happened.

Within thirty minutes, I was back in Bloom's office.

"My dick is good. *Exceptional* dick," he said, stone-faced.

"What did he find?" I asked, matching his seriousness.

"Aside from *Josiah's* Infiniti ..." Bloom took a deep breath and looked at his notes. He held one sheet of paper slightly toward him as he read. "One, Elsie Morton, formerly known as Sydney Porter, most recently had a permanent residence with Mark Wallace at 1111 Walker Lane in Denver." He looked at me. "Are you ready for what's next?"

"Yes," I said, swallowing.

"You sure?"

I motioned for him to continue.

"Okay, then."

He continued reading. "Credible sources indicate that any trace of Sydney Porter's existence terminated following a murder that occurred in Lake Forest, a posh northern suburb of Chicago. The homicide victim, Sergei Kalishav, was a prominent member of the Russian bratva—that's their mafia."

I'd known some of this, but I wondered how much more the P.I. had found. My heart was in my throat, and I felt faint.

He kept reading.

"Sydney Porter was held at a safe house in connection with the murders. She wasn't yet being treated as a suspect, but she was being protected from the bratva." Bloom cleared his throat and turned the page. "This is where it gets crazy, if it wasn't already crazy enough for you." I blinked rapidly. He continued. "According to these same sources, two federal Marshals were holding Ms. Porter for questioning. The agents were scheduled to be relieved by two additional agents on the evening of July seventeenth. That exchange never took place because all four agents were murdered. And before anyone arrived on the scene, Sydney Porter had escaped."

"There's no way," I said, before he could say anything else. "She couldn't have done that."

Bloom leaned back in his chair. "She didn't even tell you her real fucking name. She's been on the run. She's probably running from the federal government and the Russian bratva. Anything she has ever said to you has been a lie."

"If she murdered the agents, then why wasn't it all over the news? Why didn't I find anything about this when I searched her name?"

He considered that. "Her safety," he said, picking up another piece of paper. "This is where it gets good … It's possible that two of the agents may have been compromised by the Russian bratva. In which case, they may have been responsible for killing two of the agents. It's possible that Sydney Porter retaliated by murdering the two agents who had been compromised."

"So, either way," I couldn't believe what I was about to say, "Elsie is a killer."

"*Sydney,*" Bloom corrected me. "Sydney Porter is a killer.

"Is there anything else?" I asked, motioning toward his stack of papers.

"Oh, yeah," he said. "My dick also believes that they have surveillance on you. They want Sydney. They'll do anything to make her answer for what she did. They'd been searching for her for more than a decade. She had apparently lived completely off the grid until she met you."

I didn't even know which statement to answer to. They had threatened my sister to get to me, to get to Elsie. They had definitely gotten to me, but I didn't know how I was supposed to give up Elsie. I didn't even know where she was.

"What in the hell should I do?" I asked.

"Are you a religious man?"

"Lutheran," I said.

He didn't hesitate. "Pray that they don't reform your face."

Forty-Eight

MARK

After leaving Bloom's office, his dry joke finally hit me: *Luther's Reformation.* That wasn't bad, but I wasn't in the mood. I had two days to produce Elsie or else I feared that they would take out my sister. Maybe me, too. I was barreling down the interstate, heading back home. The sky was clear overhead, but it looked like it was snowing in the mountains.

I had no radio playing, only the voices inside my mind.

I didn't have any idea what I could do to protect my sister. Maybe choose a woman with less baggage. Or maybe if Elsie hadn't left me to fend for myself.

If she had just turned herself over to them, she could have

avoided all of this. Or maybe if she hadn't killed Russian mafia members in the first place. Was that really such a major thing to ask of someone?

She was ultimately to blame.

Yet we were together. I probably would have felt just as guilty if she had turned herself over and died. Maybe she didn't realize they were as close as they were and was trying to protect me by leaving? Who knows?

I stomped on the gas in frustration, weaving in and out of cars. I think I'd topped 100 at some point, but my eyes were too blurry to know for sure. Thankfully, I'd avoided crashing into anyone. I made it to our exit in record time.

It all made sense—why Elsie had been so reluctant in the beginning. Why she had been so guarded about her past. Why she had lied about Arapahoe. She probably didn't even work, or if she did, she probably had another identity. Who knows how many different names she had used?

But why in the hell did she drive a high-priced, Infiniti SUV? It wasn't close to practical and it stood out like crazy, even in our neighborhood. If she wasn't even going to work, where did she drive it to? Starbucks? Why? I felt like I was missing something, so was Bloom and the investigator.

But what?

After parking, I triple-checked my surroundings before exiting my car. I feared that the bratva would snipe me or they would have my door rigged to explode when I turned the handle.

That was the last thing that I needed to think about.

Maybe I shouldn't have driven back out here. I didn't know where else to go. I didn't want to go back to St. Louis and draw attention to more family members.

I made it back inside my apartment, safe from any explosions. I immediately went into the bedroom and closed the blinds, pulling the curtains shut.

Forty-Nine

ELSIE

In my new Airbnb, I didn't sleep much that night. Instead, I cried. And then I cried some more. It really didn't seem fair how one decision could have taken so much from me. This should have been an amazing time in my life. I'd be out of med school, probably finished with my residency. I'd have a career, maybe even a family. I should have been living in a comfortable house in a comfortable suburb, visiting my parents on the weekend and going out for dinner and drinks on beautiful patios. Traveling all over the world.

I'd experienced a fraction of that with Mark. I was just beginning to feel like I was living a semblance of a normal life.

Finally. But once again, that one decision from my past had come back with one phone call.

I hadn't known how to react. Should I have told more to Mark? Would that have made any difference? Would Mark have gone headstrong into the arms of the bratva to fight for me? I hadn't wanted to subject him to that.

I'd hoped that if I left before they got too close, that I would protect Mark. It was so stupid of me to get involved with someone and endanger them. It was my problem. I shouldn't have gotten him involved in my messy life.

Or maybe I was simply used to running. And maybe my life had also made me selfish. Maybe, in some way, I hadn't gotten as close to Mark as most other people do when they meet someone. Maybe I'd wanted to leave that emotional door open so I could simply leave and not feel so bad about it.

But I definitely missed Mark, almost immediately after leaving that day. What I wouldn't have given to return to 1111 Walker Street and hop into bed with Mark, to cuddle up in his arms and let the rest of the world pass by.

I'd never get my twenties back, but I at least wanted to get back what I had in that suburban home with Mark. For once, since maybe back in high school, I'd felt truly fulfilled and content with my life.

Then again, when I was in high school, I felt suffocated by expectations. Looking back, I'm surprised that I don't know why I was so critical. I guess that's kind of what kids and teenagers do. But then it resulted in most of my rebellion.

Then again, I would have grown out of that and been fine if Julia hadn't died. In my head, all of my actions seemed right at the time. But I definitely hadn't been in the right frame of mind after Julia died.

I couldn't really think about that anymore. No, all I could think was what I could do now. In the present.

I needed to make sure that we survived this. I needed to find some way to protect Mark and make up for running away and leaving him alone.

Mark was the closest thing that I'd had to real family since I'd been on the road. There were random friends along the way—some of them a little closer than others, but I was usually moving around quite a bit.

I needed to find Mark. I needed to somehow resolve this. The trouble was, I just didn't know how.

I knew if I tried to turn myself over to the bratva that I would just be killed. Mark would probably also be killed as some kind of retribution.

I needed to be far enough away yet close enough that if something happened, I could be there to help Mark. That night back in Chicago, I was lucky that there were only two bratva members. Even then, I barely survived. If I'd missed with any of my shots, I would have died.

I tried to train more since then. I tried to get better with the weapons just in case, but I could still easily be outnumbered. That's what scared me most. It also didn't help that I couldn't exactly go to the authorities because I didn't exist, at least not who I was. And ultimately, I had also killed two agents. I was sure that they were the bratva in disguise, but they were wearing official uniforms so I couldn't be sure. Either way, there were four people dead. Obviously, I was the only one who had survived. I needed to be sure that my innocence was secure.

At some point, I had finally stopped crying. I had to. Crying wasn't going to help me. It wasn't going to do anything positive for me. I needed to somehow get to sleep. I needed a rejuvenated mind to develop a strategy for moving forward.

For now, it seemed like all I could do was wait to see what happened. I'd sketched out plans for killing Yuri, while I was in a rage up in the mountains, but I needed more backup and support. I reasoned that Yuri would have plenty of protection and firepower.

I finally fell asleep. I was going to need my rest for the action that was coming.

Fifty

MARK

I stayed in my apartment the next day. I wasn't sure if that was better or worse than going out. I didn't want to risk running into that guy again. The worst part was that he knew exactly where I lived. He had stood in front of my door.

I thought about calling the cops, but I didn't. Not yet. Once again, I wasn't sure what they would be able to do. Nothing had happened other than a vague threat. I also had no proof.

Plus, I still wasn't sure if they would tie Elsie to Horace's death. Or me. Or both of us.

Later that day, Attorney Bloom called. I'd actually kept him kind of busy—between him and the investigator.

"This might be good news," he said.

"Yeah?" I said. "What's going on?" I would take any good news that I could at this point.

"Elsie's Infiniti that they found? Our sources indicate that it has been checked for prints, but they haven't found any. They're assuming that it was swept and/or someone had used gloves while placing Horace's body inside. Horace didn't die in the vehicle. They're almost sure of that."

"Okay," I said. "So, what does that mean?"

I heard him take a deep breath. "It means that they cannot tie Horace's death to Elsie or Sydney. I'd assumed that they might be able to match Sydney's prints since she was surely fingerprinted when the Federal Marshals took her to the safehouse. She should be in the system. That would have resulted in chaos. I'm not sure how much they would have reported considering she's technically still needing protection from the bratva. And hell, maybe they did find her prints. Maybe they are simply trying to protect her. They could know more than we do, especially if the Feds are more involved."

He continued. "It seems like the bratva was trying to send a compound message with this slaying. How are you holding up over there?"

"They came by my house and told me that I have two days to produce Elsie."

"Shit, that good?" He laughed in disbelief. "I'd tell you to call the cops, but I'm not sure how much they would do, especially considering that they suspect you in Horace's death. If they knew that was Elsie's vehicle, it might make it worse. The false registration makes it look like you were both into some shady fucking shit. You see that, right? Anyway, man, I'd hang low. Hopefully, you're strapped. You need to protect yourself. I don't think they'd risk killing you. They're trying to draw Elsie—or *Sydney*—out. If they kill you, she's gone and they won't ever find her. They're too close to risk that."

"Yeah, and I have no idea where she's at."

Bloom was surprisingly quiet for a moment, but then he sprung back to life. "Another thing, that Josiah Wilkins that the car was registered to?"

"Yeah? What about him?" I said, bracing myself for the news. I was assuming that he had also been found dead.

"Well, he supposedly died a few years ago, on a hot summer night back in Chicago. Not sure if there's any connection here or not. My dick is looking into it."

"Great," I said, wondering where that might lead.

"Sorry, man, but I need to get ready for another client. We'll need to discuss further payment if this continues. I'm trying to help you out as much as I can. This situation is just fucked."

"Thanks, I appreciate it."

He told me to take care and once again, I was alone.

I considered what my attorney had told me. I wondered how the bratva had even acquired Elsie's car. If they had it, then wouldn't they also have her? Maybe she had stashed it, like the investigator thought. That made the most sense. Otherwise, they wouldn't have still been asking me to produce her.

It just made me worry about her even more. Where had she been hiding out over the last several days? Before that, she had been in our bed … It's crazy how drastically things can change in such a short period of time.

After driving back to our apartment, I thought about making another omelet. I feared that this one would also be full of tears, but I needed to eat something. I couldn't remember the last time that I'd had a substantive meal that consisted more of picking up Smashburger or Chipotle. *My oatmeal.*

I compromised and had a large glass of water. It almost hurt to swallow. I didn't realize how dry I had been.

A little before bed, I made the mistake of glancing outside the window. I wasn't sure it would have mattered either way. I'd rather it happened this way than the man beating down my door.

The same guy was standing on the street, his face illuminated by the streetlight. It was colder than yesterday, but he didn't seem to mind.

He stared back at me with one finger in the air.

"One day," he mimed. "One day."

And with that, just like the day before, he took off. I debated chasing him down the street, but I quickly rejected that idea. He would pummel me, no doubt about it. I wasn't a slouch, but he had at least fifty pounds on me. Probably fifty pounds of pure muscle.

With that, I called my sister, just to check in. I needed to know that they were all safe.

And they were. Perfectly fine. My sister was still a little rattled, but other than that, she was okay.

"Be extra safe tomorrow," I had said.

"Why?" she asked, probably holding her breath.

I explained the guy coming around my house. She panicked, but I'd said, "I'm sure they just want me. They just put that note under the door to scare me, to make me worry about you."

That may have smoothed over her fear, just a little.

I'd added, "But please, just be careful."

The countdown had been for my sister. I felt responsible, but I wasn't sure what more I could have done.

Fifty-One

MARK

The next day went about as well as could be expected, considering the threats from the Russian bratva, Elsie still missing, and everything else that had happened, including Horace's death. Thankfully, at least I still hadn't been arrested for doing anything with Ally. Not that I had, but I didn't know what she might try to say. And if they would believe her story.

The call came. Earlier than I'd expected, but maybe they'd figured that her guard would be down in the morning.

"Mark," Melissa said, her voice coming out different than I'd ever heard it. I immediately knew something was wrong.

"You okay?" I asked.

"Someone is following me," she said, barely above a whisper, her voice shrouded in fear. "I'm scared. What do I do?"

Damn.

They really were pulling my sister into this. I'd hoped that they were just trying to scare me. I now knew that it hadn't been a hollow threat, but what was I supposed to do?

"We'll look into it," was the only response I'd received, from both the Chicago and Edwardsville police. They really didn't have much to go on.

"It's going to be okay. Call the cops," I said. "9-1-1. Tell them where you're at. Where are you—"

She cut me off, screaming into the phone. There was a loud bang, but it didn't sound like a gunshot. Her screaming was now further away. Maybe she had dropped her phone.

"Mel!" I yelled, "Melissa!"

She didn't respond. I didn't hear any more screaming.

Nothing at all.

I looked at my phone. The call was still connected.

Finally, a voice spoke on the other end.

"Hope you said goodbye."

"Melissa!" I yelled. The man laughed. "If you want me, come get me! You know where I'm at! You've got to believe me! I have no idea where Elsie is!"

"We will see. You have a niece and nephew, no?"

"Don't fucking touch them. If you—"

The man ended the call.

Later that day, I had another call.

Mom.

I swallowed. My mom seldom called me. Considering what had happened during the call with my sister, I didn't want to answer. I felt a strong sense of foreboding as I pressed accept on my steering wheel.

"Hello," I said.

"Mark," she said, sniffling.

Daggers carved my stomach. My breathing stopped.

I took a deep breath. "What is it?"

"Melissa."

It didn't need to be said, but I knew it would. I braced myself as I pulled into a Wendy's parking lot. My eyes began to flood. Even though I'd braced myself, even though I already knew, my mom's next words punched me in the stomach.

"She's in the hospital." Long silence. "Mark?"

I took a second to compose myself. "I'll be right there."

"Hurry. I love you."

"Love you too, Mom."

I'd said that I'd be right there, but I wouldn't be.

Fifty-Two

MARK

I booked the next flight out of Denver, but it wasn't until the next morning. Later that afternoon, Detective Brighton called. He asked if I'd be able to come in and speak with them. I politely declined. I didn't even mention my sister's accident. He said that he could make life difficult for me. I couldn't even hold back my incredulous laugh. I was surprised that I could even laugh at the time. I'd hung up on him.

He'd tried calling me again, but I didn't answer. I didn't have to talk to him, and hopefully, I'd never need to again.

Everything was in slow motion. People say that, but you never really experience the feeling until crap really hits the fan.

Just like I'd experienced during the car crash that took Riley's life. But this experience had been painfully drawn out over several, gut-wrenching days. What's crazier is that the rest of the world continues to move at their normal clip.

I'd been moving in slow motion since Elsie left, but this was like four times slow motion. And the carnage was piling up. First, Horace, and now, my sister.

In the coming hours, I'd wonder how I could have let my guard down so much. Elsie had been missing for a week. It had led me on a wild chase that culminated with the news that she had shot and killed Federal Marshals. Maybe she had acted in self-defense, maybe not. I knew that the Russian bratva had also been involved. But what was I supposed to have done? Should I have run off into the mountains? Hopped a flight to Europe? I realize that I had the money to start fresh somewhere. But Elsie was still here, somewhere. *Maybe.*

I'd decided, without much consideration, to stay in my apartment on Walker Street. *Our* apartment.

The next morning, I'd be on my way to St. Louis. Hopefully, I wouldn't be leading the bratva to the rest of my family. Then again, if they'd found my sister without my help, then they probably already knew where everyone else lived.

I'd been watching a little TV, if you could call it that. I wasn't really watching and it wasn't really TV—just another pointless show to dull and program the minds of the masses. As a teacher, maybe I'm biased in that regard. I just felt myself becoming more and more bitter the longer this played out.

I flipped off the TV. The ensuing quietness gave me pause. It seemed far too quiet. A slight hum from my plugged-in laptop, but other than that, nothing. No cars passing on the street—not completely unusual at this hour—or anything else.

Maybe I was paranoid.

I crept down the hall and toward the bedroom, the floorboards creaking beneath my feet. I'd wanted to grab one of my golf clubs, but they were in the storage room beneath the stairs.

I'd immediately gone from letting my guard down to being insanely paranoid. I entered my bedroom. I took a deep breath and exhaled. Nobody was in here waiting for me. I checked under the bed just to make sure.

Nope. Nobody.

"Pull it together, Mark," I said, walking over to the window. I pulled the curtains back for the first time in a while. My eyes found Ally's house. Her curtains were actually open, to what I presumed was her living room downstairs. I'd been in that room, but the memory wasn't there.

It looked like a candle might have been burning. She was probably having a relaxing night, curled up with a book.

Just when I was about to turn away, she appeared in front of the window. She actually started to wave, but she held a curious expression.

I raised my hand to wave back, remembering our *interesting* exchange in the hallway of the high school. But then her eyes shot wide. Her hand covered her mouth. She finally pointed and shouted something, maybe my name.

My focus had zeroed in on her, but I finally caught a figure moving toward me in the window's reflection.

By the time I turned around, it was too late.

Fifty-Three

ELSIE

My phone continued to ring, but I just looked at it. It was the same number as before, back when I realized that it had all escalated. How had this all happened so quickly? I didn't want to answer because I already knew what he was going to say.

The phone stopped ringing for a few seconds, but then it rang again, cutting through me. The process repeated two more times until I finally answered.

"Hello?"

"Sydney." A brief pause. "We have Mark."

One tear fell and then another. I didn't say anything, there was nothing to say.

"A life for a life. Meet at the cabin where you stayed before. A few days ago, I believe."

My skin crawled. Had they known where I'd been hiding? And if so, how? But it's not like it mattered.

"Sydney, did you hear?"

"Yeah," I squeaked, surprised at my own voice.

"Yeah?"

"Yes. Yes, I will be there."

"You might want to hurry. Your man does not look good. See you soon, Sydney."

I wanted to yell at him. I wanted to scream that my name was Elsie, not Sydney. Sydney had died all of those years ago, along with any chance that I'd had at a normal life. Was it really my fault? Should I have just rolled over and taken it?

I opened the door to leave my Airbnb, coming face-to-face with a man who had enjoyed making Mark's life hell.

Fifty-Four

ELSIE

After nearly running into the man, I pulled back. Beneath his navy jacket, I could see that a shoulder holster held a gun.

"You," I said. "I know you. What are you doing here?"

"Sydney Porter," he said. "I've been keeping an eye on you and Mark."

"You're the music teacher who calls him Marky Mark?"

The corners of his lips raised slightly. "Yeah, that's right. I'm Kyle Bellamy. I'm a Federal Marshal. I've been on your case for some time now."

No way. I couldn't believe it. He looked so young. Had they been secretly monitoring me?

"They have him!" I said, finally reorienting myself. "We need to get out there. He's in a cabin off of 119."

"I know, I know," Kyle said. "I have an Explorer out front. We were waiting for confirmation. We will infiltrate the cabin and bring him out."

"They said a life for a life. I was going to turn myself over to them," I said. "What if they kill him when your team arrives? We can't risk that!"

He explained their plan and we were off.

I wanted to trust the Marshal, but my previous experience had made me so leery. I wanted to see Bellamy as Swinton and less like the other two that had barged into the safe house. I knew they weren't actually agents, but how did I know for sure that Bellamy was?

It would be a stretch to think that he was a bratva member posing as a Marshal who also posed as a substitute music teacher. Okay, maybe I could trust him. That kind of twist of fate would be a little too ridiculous, even for my life.

Fifty-Five

ELSIE

Why couldn't this have happened in the summer, I thought, as the Explorer lumbered through the narrow highway leading out to the cabin. The snow was falling harder than it had on the night that Charles had shown up. The higher elevations were supposed to get buried with a few feet by tomorrow afternoon. The cabin would get a foot or more.

I thought back to the last time I'd been out there, how Charles had scared the crap out of me when he busted in and chased me outside into the blizzard.

Except this time, we were prepared for the brutal weather. Bellamy had given me some of the warmest thermal layers that

I had ever worn. I guess working as a U.S. Marshal had some sweet perks.

I tried so hard not to think about the previous Marshals that I'd known. I could still hear their screams.

Swinton and Reich.

Now, I needed to be more worried about getting Mark out of there alive. If I needed to, I'd gladly sacrifice myself for him, but the Marshals weren't going to let me do that. And in the end, I realized that my death might be even harder for Mark to live with. In a way, it might even be more selfish.

"Hey," Bellamy said, looking back at me from the passenger seat. "Are you sure you want to come out here?"

"It's a little too late to turn around now, isn't it?" I smirked.

"Good point," he said. Turning to look through the front window. "This is insanity, but it's all worth it to bring Marky Mark back to us."

That made me smile. Mark would always come home bitching about the music teacher making Marky Mark references.

"Are you boys ready? We are T-minus-five. We will disembark and hike from behind. The cabin will likely be fortified in some way. Expect ten to fifteen men, maybe more, but probably on the lower end."

My heart was racing. Kyle made it sound like they were going to war with the Kalishav bratva.

"Do you really think there will be that many people guarding him? I was going to come by myself."

Kyle looked back, parting his lips slightly, then exhaling.

"This is the Kalishav bratva. You took three of theirs, including family. Blood is still owed."

That gave me goosebumps, even though I knew as much. I had been so young. There must have been another way to get out of that mess, but I hadn't seen one. I'd only seen rage and the need for vengeance after Julia's death.

I closed my eyes and willed the world away.

Bellamy said, "It's time. Stay inside with these two."

And then he was off, joined by several others.

I wasn't sure how many Explorers had followed ours. There was one in front and at least one behind.

It had all happened so fast, and it was exactly the same as back then. Two Federal Marshals ordered to protect me. The Russian bratva threatening once again.

This time I was older, but I was just as scared, if not more so. Youth had given me feelings of invincibility.

But now, I realized just how vulnerable I was, and how helpless Mark must have felt inside the cabin. I didn't even want to imagine what they might have been doing to him.

Within minutes, I heard the first shots. They somehow sounded both far away and close. A couple of pops and then what sounded like rapid fire. I needed to find some way to get up there. I needed to know what was happening.

Fifty-Six

United States Marshal, Kyle Bellamy, had charged up the side of the mountain, thankful that they had all packed their snowshoes. The snow would have made the hike impossible without them. Thankfully, there weren't any real elevation gains from where they had parked. Just a lot of snow.

They were quiet as they approached, still two hundred yards out. And that's when the first shots were fired, the ones that Elsie had heard from the Explorer. Bellamy prayed that she would stay put, but he wasn't holding his breath.

Two shots had been fired toward them. He wondered how many of their men were hidden in the woods, just waiting for the right second to unleash a flurry of bullets upon them.

And then he heard the ripple of automatic gunfire and watched the snow shoot into the air. Bullets sprayed not more than thirty yards from him.

He dove behind a tree, hoping that it was between him and the bratva.

Another round of gunfire, all of it coming from just outside of the cabin. He didn't know how they would have any chance of infiltrating the cabin.

He wasn't sure if he should have told Elsie who was actually inside the cabin. He wasn't sure it would have served any positive purpose.

Fifty-Seven

MARK

When I regained consciousness, I couldn't see anything. I couldn't move anything. I caught a draft. I had to be close to a window or in a poorly insulated building. The strong scent of lumber made me wonder if I was in a cabin.

The last thing I'd remembered was turning around into a large mass. It must have been a body. I wasn't even sure how they had knocked me out. I didn't remember anything after turning around.

It was obvious that someone had captured me. I assumed that it was the Russian bratva that I had heard so much about. I thought of Horace and Julia. I wondered if I was about to meet their same fate. I also couldn't help but wonder if Elsie was either somehow behind it or if she was innocent.

She *had* to be innocent. I knew her better than that.

I bit back the snide rebuttal that was forming in the back of my mind because I didn't really know her.

I finally heard voices in the other room. They were muffled, but it didn't sound like they were speaking English. I could have already guessed as much.

Hearing was about the only thing I could do. In addition to blindfolding me, they had gagged me. They had also bound my wrists behind my back and tied my legs to a chair.

If I got enough propulsion, could I throw my body up from the chair? When the voices had cleared the area, I rocked back and forth, testing my theory.

I thought it might work, but if there was more than one person in or around the cabin, I wouldn't get far.

Then the gunfire erupted, nearly blowing out my eardrums. The shot had to have come from just outside the cabin.

Without being able to see or move, I couldn't describe how helpless I felt. If a stray bullet hit me—or even one directed at me, I'd be dead without even knowing what happened.

Each time I heard a shot, I mentally prepared for the end. The scent of the gunfire had quickly overwhelmed the lumber.

Suddenly, two sets of footfalls stormed into the room, rushing toward me.

"Your girl brought trouble," a man said. "That is no good for her. Or you. No mind. We will make her watch."

I thought I might have been in range if I tried to throw myself at the man, but it wouldn't have done any good. It might have been an instant death sentence rather than painfully dragging it out like this.

That might have been better.

And then the rapid fire started. The man shuffled away, opening and closing the door.

The other person lingered in the room. I heard someone step right behind me. I was bracing for a gunshot to the head, a knife to the throat, punch to the stomach. Something.

I felt the sensation of the person leaning toward me. I felt the breath, hot on my ear. And then I was slapped hard, two times across the cheek.

Fifty-Eight

ELSIE

I wasn't going to stay in the Explorer. There was no way in hell. I'd gone to war with these guys before, and I was going to do it again. I wondered if any of these other guys had ever killed one of the bratva. I'd killed three of them.

Not that I was proud of that. It had destroyed my life.

But I was going to go down fighting to get my life back— my personal freedom and my life with Mark. It was time to stop running away from them.

Marshal Bellamy had outfitted me in combat gear to protect me in a worst-case scenario. I had the body armor, and there was still plenty of firepower in the vehicle.

The war continued on the snow-covered incline above us. I thought of Bellamy, and I hoped that he was getting along okay. He had been so kind.

When I made the decision to leave, it came without much of a diversion. I simply grabbed a gun and took off. They tried to pull me back, but I wasn't going to be denied.

I opened the door quietly and looked back at them.

"Don't draw attention to us," I said. I grabbed a pair of snowshoes, and I left the door slightly cracked. With my back up against the Explorer, I finagled the contraptions over my boots, then I high-stepped through the snow.

I glanced back toward the Explorer, two men had stepped outside, guns drawn. I hoped they were coming along to provide cover, but who knows.

If anything, this was smart. It would give us more of a chance. I didn't know what would happen if we ran out of men against them. I guess that's where we came in, as a last-case scenario, or maybe there were reinforcements on their way.

I couldn't think of that. We wouldn't need them.

A man yelled out in pain up ahead. He had been shot. He was probably still five hundred feet away, but I needed to be vigilant.

I thought of the night I ran through the trees, away from the bloodbath in the safehouse. I'd run so fast through those trees, but now, I was barely trudging through the snow-covered forest.

I'd been running away for so long. Even if they shot me dead, at least I wouldn't be running away anymore.

I was now running directly into the fire in a desperate attempt to salvage some normalcy.

And there was plenty of fire. Based on the gunshots, it sounded like a full-blown war was raging up ahead.

I stumbled in the snow, bracing myself against a tree. Hiking up the hill would have been hard enough if there wasn't any snow, but this was torture.

I needed to keep going.

I pushed myself away from the tree and onward, amid the cries and the popping of gunshots. Most of the action was still way up ahead, but it seemed like it was moving closer to me. I feared that the Kalishav bratva had gained an advantage and pushed our line back.

If so, how much longer would I be alive?

Fifty-Nine

The two Marshals had been fully prepared for Elsie to leave. There wasn't much they could do. They could only protect her so much, and that's how it had been for the last decade-plus. After she had moved twenty yards from the vehicle, they followed her for protection.

Kyle Bellamy was getting close to the cabin, but they had suffered a great loss. By his count, four of his partners had been gunned down. It could have easily been him. He had heard several bullets whizz by his head, cutting through the snowfall.

Yet he pressed on. This was exactly what he had signed up for. He loved every minute of it, and if it was his time to go, then he would go down fighting and trying to protect others.

Sixty

ELSIE

The fighting had moved toward the front of the cabin. Now, I thought that Kyle and the other agents were actually gaining ground. I wanted to provide more cover. I was on my way around the back of the cabin when I stopped short. Through the window, the same window I had pushed open just a few days before, I saw Mark.

I whispered his name, knowing that he couldn't hear me. I stumbled toward the window, making myself vulnerable.

Aside from Mark, the room looked unoccupied. If anyone else was still inside the cabin, then they were surely more interested in protecting the front door from the advancing Marshals.

I took my glove off and scraped the snow and ice away from the glass. I thought Mark had heard it. He stiffened just a little.

I scraped just a little more.

I'd taken a few small steps away from the window when a large hand came down on my shoulder.

Sixty-One

ELSIE

"Hey," Bellamy said, turning me slightly. "You okay?"

After the initial panic of his hand hitting my shoulder, I'd calmed back down. I'd thought I was finished.

I nodded. "Yeah."

"Let's move," he said.

Bellamy and I inched toward the front door of the cabin. Another Marshal—Williams—was on the other side. My legs were burning like crazy. It would have been easy to collapse onto the ground, but the adrenaline had taken over.

It was now or never.

I now knew that Mark was inside. And he was alive. I hadn't

seen anyone else in the room with him, but I knew that Yuri and maybe others had to be inside.

Bellamy and Williams seemed set on going in through the front door, providing cover along the way. I wondered if that would be the best way. I wasn't sure.

I knew that whoever was in there would be waiting on the other side. They might be sitting ducks.

I'd considered trying to rescue Mark through the window, but we would be going in blind. Plus, I knew that the window scraped loudly, making a lot of noise that would surely give them all away and get them killed.

Unless …

Some kind of a diversion might be the best way. *Naturally.* I thought back to Chicago and how I had taken out the first man who had entered the bedroom.

We had no idea how many were inside. Maybe we really needed to all stick together to have the best odds.

I heard Bellamy tell Williams that backup was coming, but I didn't want to take the chance that the remaining bratva would get desperate when backed up like this. They might go ahead and kill Mark, to at least take something away from me, even if they might give up on killing me.

We couldn't afford to wait. We couldn't let that happen.

Suddenly, Williams reached for the door just to see if it would open. My heartbeat intensified. We were in motion. One way or another, this mission was going to be resolved soon.

Williams pushed the door.

It was unlocked. He shoved it open while getting down. They hadn't yet entered.

I waited for the cascade of gunshots, but they didn't come. Not yet. My heart was racing wildly. I was so close to Mark. He was just on the other side of the cabin wall. We were too close to a reunion for it not to happen.

Once again, I had a flashback to the compromised Marshals entering the bedroom where I cut them down. I remembered how just a little noise, even when someone is focused, can divert their attention just enough to let down their guard. All I'd done then was toss a pen against the window on the other side of the room. That had been enough.

But now ...

I grabbed Bellamy's shoulder, pulling him back a little, and said, "Go. I'll take the window."

He gave me a stern look. A questioning look, but then he finally nodded. He must have remembered that I had successfully battled the bratva before, and that I had successfully avoided them for more than a decade.

I was just going with my gut instinct. Again. Hopefully, it would help me like it did back in Chicago. I didn't know if it was the right thing to do.

God be damned if I was going to cower behind the Marshals or take off running like I'd already run so much. I was going to go through the window, or at least open it. Maybe the scraping noise would provide the necessary diversion to give us a chance of beating them.

But for all I knew, someone was waiting right under the window for me to do it. I thought I'd be able to see someone lying in wait, but maybe not. It would be a smart move to leave Mark in clear view to draw me into the room. Then again, I'd already stood next to the window without anything happening.

At least I'd been in the room before—the entire cabin. I knew the layout, just as I'd known the layout of the safehouse back in Chicago.

The Marshals finally turned to enter the cabin. I knew that everything could change within a few seconds.

We could all be dead so quickly.

I just needed to get to Mark. That was my burning drive and desire. Ultimately, Mark was the reason why I had risked coming down from the mountains and trying to live a normal life.

The Marshals advanced into the cabin, but I still hadn't heard anything yet. The cabin wasn't very big. I didn't know where the rest of the bratva could be hiding. Maybe they had fled the cabin when the Marshals got close.

Nope. Just then, I heard the shots. One, then two.

And that was my cue. I pushed the window open hard. It scraped so loudly as it went up. I heard Mark try to murmur something against the gag.

My heart was beating wildly, my stomach was tight. I frantically searched the room, still not seeing anything.

To get into the room, I'd have to hoist myself up and then over, and in the process, I'd be vulnerable. I didn't know if I'd be able to keep holding the gun *and* keep it aimed over the room.

Before I could make the decision, I felt someone come up from behind me. I must not have heard them thanks to the snowfall muffling their movements.

But someone was definitely behind me. And then a gun was pushed into my side.

Sixty-Two

ELSIE

I slowly turned around. Mark's student, Ally, stared back, shaking slightly. I wasn't sure if it was because of the cold or fear.

"Don't move," she said, softly. "Don't make a sound or I'll kill you, and then I'll kill Mark."

"Ally, what are you doing here?" I whispered.

"Drop your gun," she said.

I complied. I had no choice. It fell from my hand and through the fresh snow, barely making a sound.

My pulse raced. My heart threatened to explode.

I needed to take her down, but I had no weapon. I could wrestle her, but the gun aimed at me negated that idea. If I dared to make any movement, she would shoot. I was at her mercy. Whenever she decided to pull the trigger, I was done. I had no options left. I could only pray for some kind of a miracle.

"Why?" I asked. "Why, Ally?"

"Nataliya," she corrected me.

"Nataliya?" I repeated, looking at her blankly.

"You murdered my dad …"

I stared blankly at her.

"I was there when it happened. When they found me, I was covered in his blood. They had to pull me away, I couldn't stop crying. I didn't want to leave him there. He was so alone. But they made me. Because of you!" Her voice raised slightly as she kept going. Each word burned as they entered my ears and registered in my brain.

Forever imprinted. At least forever wouldn't last long.

"Nataliya, I'm so—" I started.

"He fucked me, you know?" Ally said, cutting me off.

"What?" I asked, my heartbeat even faster now. "I did not."

"Mark. He fucked me. Actually, we made love."

"No," I said, shaking my head.

I spied someone coming up from behind Ally. I just hoped that he would get to her before Ally decided to pull the trigger and end my life.

I returned my focus to Ally.

She said, "Yes, we did, and it was so amazing." Her eyes sparkled. She was so beautiful. I felt a sting of jealousy, even when I was most concerned about the gun pointed in my face.

In a way, she had already shot me.

My eyes flicked just to the side of her face again. I could now see that it was Bellamy, closing in, but he was still far away. Probably too far. They must have cleared out the inside and he was circling back for me.

"Now, you must die for what you did to my dad," Ally said. "I'm sorry …. *Aunt* Elsie." She grinned. An evil grin. And then she took a deep breath, taking aim.

I closed my eyes.

Sixty-Three

ELSIE

Bellamy must have lunged at her. I heard a slight grunt and then the sound of Bellamy's body crashing into Ally.

And then a loud gunshot.

I was afraid to open my eyes. I didn't think I'd been shot, but the gun being fired so close to my head was deafening. All I could hear was a loud hum.

When I finally opened my eyes, Bellamy had Ally pinned to the ground, face down in the snowpack.

"Come on, help me get her inside," he said. At least that's what I thought he'd said.

I nodded, trying to snap myself back into coherence.

We stood Ally up. She must have been in a daze or simply felt too defeated to say anything or put up a fight.

"She didn't have sex with Mark," Bellamy said, his hand on my shoulder.

I turned toward him, narrowing my eyes.

Ally showed some life again. She protested, "Yes, we did. The night after the poker game. He came over and bent me over my couch. He pulled my hair while—"

"No," Bellamy said. "He didn't do any of that. You talked to him on the sidewalk, but he walked away from you."

I unclenched my jaw.

"Yes, he did. He fucked me," Ally said, grinning. "Hard."

Bellamy began his rebuttal, but I interrupted him. "This isn't important right now. We need to get inside. Did you clear the cabin?" I asked.

"Not quite," Bellamy said. "I came back outside for you when I heard Ally yelling. Williams is down. I think it's just me and you now. I don't know who's left inside. Our backup should be here any minute."

"In Mark's room?" I asked. "I didn't see anyone."

"We didn't get to the other room, either," Bellamy said, exhaling. "We took several of them down."

I wondered if the bratva had more reinforcements behind the other door, but they surely would have come out when they heard the shots. I hoped that we would be able to take them.

We walked Ally into the cabin. I kept my eyes peeled, scanning the room, recognizing that one of the bedroom doors was now open. I glanced at Ally, she seemed to be looking toward the closed door leading to Mark's room. That made me think again of what she had said …

I couldn't think about that now.

"Let's get Mark," Bellamy said, pointing toward the door.

I took that as a cue to open it. I pulled the door open and looked at Mark.

His eyes were wild with fear.

Sixty-Four

ELSIE

Bellamy launched himself into the room, leaving Ally to crumple to the ground. It seemed that she was all out of fight.

"Hands raised! Hands raised!" Bellamy said.

The man didn't need to comply because his hands were already in the air. He stepped away from Mark. No weapon. At least not one at his imminent disposal. He was a large man, an older man.

It was Yuri Kalishav. His lips were in a straight line.

"Don't move," Bellamy shouted, gun raised. With his free hand, he spoke into his walkie, "We have *him*. In the cabin. Yuri Kalishav. Cabin is clear."

Yuri only stared at Bellamy, and then swung his eyes to me.

"Sydney Porter," he said. "Or whatever your name is." He flicked his hand in the air. "You caused my family great pain. You killed both of my sons. And you killed my nephew."

"I killed one of your sons because he killed Julia."

"Accident," he said, but I wasn't sure if he believed it. "What you did was no accident. You robbed me of my sons, and you robbed a little girl of her father. My little rabbit. And my other son and my nephew, you shot after."

The compromised Marshals. "They were going to kill me. They killed the other two Marshals. The Marshals were innocent!"

Bellamy interjected. "Yuri Kalishav, I am placing you under arrest for a litany of crimes."

Yuri closed his eyes and laughed. It was a low, sad noise that rumbled through us.

"I'm not going anywhere. I'm an old man. My family is finished. There is no point to continue to live."

From nowhere, two other Marshals entered the cabin. They had their guns raised. I had flashbacks. I was prepared to raise my gun and shoot, but I didn't.

Thankfully.

I quickly realized that their guns were locked on the bratva boss. Bellamy closed in, cuffs in tow. The other Marshals flanked him on each side.

"Yuri, don't try anything," Bellamy said, slowing his advance yet remaining cautious. "Put your hands behind your back … Do it now!"

Yuri Kalishav shook his head and grabbed for his gun, drawing it, but not firing. It didn't matter.

One agent shot, and then another. Two more bullets tore through Yuri's chest.

Yuri smiled as he fell to the ground.

I gasped. His body rocked the cabin floor. The blood seeped from his chest and forehead.

Ally finally snapped out of her daze. She lunged toward her grandpa, screaming.

Bellamy leapt forward, trying to pull her back, but she swung on him, striking him in the face. Bellamy exercised considerable restraint and safely corralled her in his arms.

Another agent quickly secured Yuri's gun, though Ally had made no attempt for it.

"*Deda!*" Ally cried. "No, not you, too! No!"

Tears streamed down her face as she tried to claw through Bellamy and back to her grandpa.

Part of me wanted to run up to her and give her a huge hug. She was my niece. *Nataliya.* Julia's daughter. A part of Julia was standing right there in front of me. But I also saw her as Ally, part of the bratva. I was assuming she had turned over our location to them and put us in danger.

But could I have even blamed her?

I'd hastily acted when I'd taken out her dad. She was left to grow up without either parent. But he was such an awful man. I'd watched him kill people, other than Julia. I'd also heard him plan other crimes that he didn't actively take part in.

Either way, it would have been a tortuous childhood for her. I honestly thought I'd given her the best chance at a healthy life. But now, I prayed for her. It was all I could do.

Marshal Bellamy said, "Nataliya Tokareva, we are placing you under arrest."

She gasped. "What? Me? For what? You just murdered my grandpa. And she killed my dad! Why aren't you arresting her?" She pointed at me.

I closed my eyes, tears seeping out. She sounded so much like Julia. Despite the black hair, I could now see the resemblance. Clear as day.

Bellamy said, with a definite tear in his voice, "You were an accessory to the kidnapping and for conspiracy to commit the murder of Sydney Porter."

I shuddered upon hearing my name, especially being so closely connected to "the murder of."

"What?" she said. "And she gets to walk free?"

"She was justified," was all that Bellamy said, looking Ally in the eyes, but then he blinked rapidly.

I wasn't sure if his blinking meant that they were going to reopen Sergei's death and charge me with murder.

Would I have to run again?

Sixty-Five

ELSIE

The rest of the night was hectic. More law enforcement arrived. They had been on their way for a while, but everything had happened so quickly. It seemed that it had taken a while, but from the moment we arrived until Ally was arrested had taken less than an hour.

Mark had passed out before I could talk to him. He was taken off the mountain in an ambulance for treatment. Now, I'd somehow found myself alone with Bellamy again.

"How did she find me?" I asked Bellamy.

He shrugged. "It turns out she spent her teenage years trying to track you down, maybe even before then. By the time she could operate a computer, our intelligence shows that she was making connections and moves to track you down. I'm not sure

291

how she did it. She knew that you had moved to Denver—with Mark. She bought a house across the street and waited. She tried to come up with a plan."

"Wait," I said. "This girl is eighteen years old, right? How in the hell did she have enough money to buy a house in our neighborhood? And that's an actual townhouse. It probably costs a lot more than our place."

"She's the beneficiary of a substantial trust," Bellamy said. "The corpus is in the tens of millions. She's been living on the amounts merely allocated as general living expenses. She receives $30,000 per month."

I could only shake my head. Under any other circumstance, I would have been shocked, but I'm not sure anything would shock me now.

"And now, after her grandfather's passing, I imagine that she'll inherit much more. Well, depending on how the criminal proceedings go."

"So why didn't she come right after me?" I asked. "It seems like she could have turned us over much quicker than she did."

Bellamy didn't even pause. "I think her plan changed when she fell for Mark. I saw the way she looked at him at school. Perhaps she thought if she could take him away from you, then maybe that would be good enough for her revenge."

At that moment, I was furious with my *niece*.

Bellamy continued. "She thought she had done it. From our intelligence, we uncovered that she sent you the first few threats, allegedly from other bratva, but she hadn't let them know where you were. Not then. Because yes, they were still actively looking for you … But anyway, she explained her situation with Mark to me one night," he said, looking away from me for a moment. "Mark had sat her down and told her that nothing could ever happen between them because he loved you. And then, I guess that's when she turned you over to the bratva. She let them know where you had been and where Mark was. They also tracked down Horace Qualls. They opted to put the pressure on Mark by assaulting his sister, but she survived, barely."

He looked away again. "By the way, someone let our vic, Mark Wallace, know that his sister will be okay."

I smiled at that, thankful that I didn't cause the death of someone else, especially Mark's sister. That meant that Ethan and Ella wouldn't have to track me down and try to kill me when they became teenagers …

Bellamy continued. "Then they decided to abduct Mark to finally draw you out."

"Why didn't you stop them when they took Mark? Why weren't you guarding our place? Why didn't you let us know?" I asked in rapid fire, as all of that suddenly dawned on me.

He looked a little guilty. "We wanted Yuri. We needed to draw *him* out. We were willing to take some risks along the way. I'm sorry."

I couldn't say much to that. I'd definitely taken my own personal risks at the expense of others. "Are there more of them? Will they still come after us?"

"Generally, yes. You would owe more blood." Bellamy

looked me dead in the eyes. "But the Kalishav bloodline has basically been eliminated. There's still family, but without Yuri, I'm not sure what will become of them. Unless …"

"Unless what?" I asked, quickly, unnerved by his tone. "All I want is a normal life. For once."

"Sorry, I was considering Nataliya. But she will surely be put away for a while. Hopefully." He went distant for a second too long. "Tell you what, we will keep an eye on everything. As always. There are still members left, but they might realize that the juice isn't worth the squeeze. Their numbers have lowered. They lost several more here today. We'll do some research and see where this family stands. In the meantime, if you need anything—new identities or whatever, we will take care of you and Marky Mark. And I'll also make sure everything gets sorted out with the school, let them know exactly what happened."

That finally made me smile, just a little. "Thank you."

Agent Bellamy nodded before walking away.

I needed to see Mark. It had been too long.

Sixty-Six

ELSIE

It was much harder than I thought it would be, facing Mark again. And I had prepared for it to be difficult. All of those nights away from Mark had been torture, especially feeling responsible for his misery, Horace's death, and the attack on his sister. He must have blamed me.

But I'd had to do what was necessary in order to survive. Did I care that Horace had died? Not if it meant that I survived. It was still sad though, it really was. Ultimately, I wondered if I was also willing to sacrifice Mark's life. How much of my running away was trying to protect him and how much was trying to protect myself? Then again, I came back for him in the end.

Because yes, I still loved him. Very much.

I thought of Ally or *Nataliya*. I really should have put the two together. She wasn't quite as transforming with her name as I had been. I tried to remember if Julia had ever called her Ally, but that was so long ago.

Julia had barely even known her daughter before she left the world. She had no idea what Ally would have grown up to become. What's sad is that Ally would have grown into a completely different woman had her mother survived.

It sucked for Ally—Julia's daughter and my honorary niece. I couldn't have even imagined, yet I could—to a degree. I hadn't lost my parents at that young of an age, but I was still young when my parents died. I didn't have much of a life after twenty-one, but any shot that Ally had of a normal life ended the night that I killed Sergei.

I tried to convince myself that it would have been worse if she had grown up with Sergei as her father. But who knows? Maybe he would have changed his ways after watching his baby girl grow. He might have even transformed into an upstanding citizen, but I robbed him of any chance of growth.

In the moment, though, he was planning and carrying out serious crimes, including murder, with Julia's daughter in the house. My best friend's blood. I couldn't take the chance that he would see the light and transform.

Maybe I'd saved Ally, after all.

I just hoped that she would make it out of this okay. If asked for sentencing recommendations, I wasn't sure what I'd say.

She needed help though. That's for sure. Anyone who had suffered to that degree definitely needs counseling … or maybe just someone to love them. Completely. Without reservation.

She'd had that with her grandpa, but now he was also gone.

I hoped that she would somehow be able to live a halfway normal life, but I had my doubts.

I wiped my face.

I realized that I was stalling, standing outside of Mark's hospital room, waiting to turn the corner and see him. I desperately wanted to, but I was so afraid of how he would react.

Finally, I walked inside the room.

Instantly, we locked eyes.

"Sydney," Mark said, still trying to get used to the sound of it. He lay in the hospital bed, hooked to an IV.

"No," I said, shaking my head, still standing several feet away from him.

Mark looked like I punched him. Maybe I shouldn't have played that card. He had been through enough.

"Call me, Elsie," I said, finally curling my lips into a smile and stepping toward him. "Elsie was my name when I met you. That's who I *always* want to be, and I want *always* to be with you."

I strode toward the bed and fell into him. He took me in his arms, running his fingers through my hair, whispering into my ear, "Els, I thought I'd lost you."

"I love you," I said. "So, so much."

"I love you, too."

For a minute, it was just us, holding each other as one. I cried into his shoulder, so grateful to be in his arms again. Knowing that it had all been worth risking. Grateful that another loved one hadn't died at my expense.

We finally pulled away from each other, and I sat on the bed next to him.

"Elsie," he said. "I have a surprise for you." He pulled out his phone. While looking down and typing, he said, "I begged her not to come. I told her it was too dangerous, but thankfully, she came—just in case there was any chance of seeing you again."

"Who?" I started, squinting my eyes, trying to think who Mark could be talking about. My mom was dead. I hadn't talked to any of my friends in more than a decade.

Suddenly, someone walked into the room.

I gasped and covered my mouth. It was my high school friend, Carina Xavier.

The tears came quickly. Carina shrieked and ran toward me, arms wide. We embraced each other hard, laughing and crying. It felt like Carina might swing me into the wall.

"Oh, my God!" I said between the tears. "My fast car-car-Carina!"

"I can't believe you remember that." Carina laughed. "I missed that name."

I smiled. "Well, I definitely don't miss *Sydney*."

Author Bio

Matt Riedle is an Estate Planning and Probate Attorney living near St. Louis. He has traveled to all fifty U.S. States and dozens of countries. He enjoys snowboarding, golf, and climbing mountains.

He has previously published the She's Toxic series:
- She's Toxic
- She Knows
- She Remains

He has also published the first book of the Garrett Daniels series:
- Box Canyon
- *Holy Communion* (Upcoming release)